SWIMMING WITH SHARKS

SWIMMING WITH SHARKS

MELISSA CRISTINA MÁRQUEZ

SCHOLASTIC INC.

Copyright © 2021 by Melissa Cristina Márquez

Illustrations by Sarah Mensinga copyright © 2021 by Scholatic Inc.

This book is being published simultaneously in hardcover by Scholastic Press.

All rights reserved. Published by Scholastic Inc., *Publishers since 1920*. SCHOLASTIC, SCHOLASTIC PRESS, and associated logos are trademarks and/or registered trademarks of Scholastic Inc.

The publisher does not have any control over and does not assume any responsibility for author or third-party websites or their content.

No part of this publication may be reproduced, stored in a retrieval system, or transmitted in any form or by any means, electronic, mechanical, photocopying, recording, or otherwise, without written permission of the publisher. For information regarding permission, write to Scholastic Inc., Attention: Permissions Department, 557 Broadway, New York, NY 10012.

This book is a work of fiction. Names, characters, places, and incidents are either the product of the author's imagination or are used fictitiously, and any resemblance to actual persons, living or dead, business establishments, events, or locales is entirely coincidental.

ISBN 978-1-338-63508-9

10 9 8 7 6 5 4 3 2 1   21 22 23 24 25

Printed in the U.S.A. 40

First printing 2021

Book design by Yaffa Jaskoll

To my family and friends—it is a joy to share a planet with you. I can never thank you for all you have done.

PROLOGUE

A sudden movement in the net caught my eye, and with another deep breath, like I saw Zev take before he went free diving, I dove underwater and kicked to get closer to the pile of stuff. There, tangled in the clear lines, was a green sea turtle, desperately wiggling back and forth to get free. I usually only saw them wriggle around so much when they were clambering onto land to sunbathe.

The stinging in my chest reminded me that I wasn't a fish and needed to take a breath. Kicking back up to the surface, I looked at the guys as I gasped and filled my lungs with air.

"There's a turtle stuck in the line!" I said. "We have to get it out!"

"It could bite you!" Feye said.

"When have you heard of a sea turtle biting someone?" I argued.

Feye looked stumped.

"Mom and Dad always say to 'do the right thing.' We can't just leave it down there to drown," I said. Sea turtles aren't like fish. They need to come up to the surface to breathe. I knew my brother wouldn't disagree with me on that. He loved animals as much as I did.

"We don't even have anything to cut it loose with, A," Feye said, sighing.

"I do!" Dilip said, rummaging in his pocket and producing a sharp knife.

Feye and I did a double take.

"What?" asked Dilip. "It's a dive knife. I have it

when I go fishing with my dad in case the line gets caught on stuff and we have to cut it off."

"That's perfect!" I said, thankful that we had run into Dilip.

"Well, nice knowing you, Dilip!" Feye said, motioning toward the pile where the sea turtle was wriggling.

"I'm not going down there! I can't hold my breath that long," Dilip said.

I grabbed the knife from him and clipped the GoPro to my shoulder so the camera could see everything. My very own animal rescue! "I'll do it," I said.

Before Feye or Dilip could stop me, I took another deep breath and swam down to the poor sea turtle, which by now had slowed its wriggling a bit. *It must be running out of oxygen. I gotta hurry!*

CHAPTER ONE

We all looked at the picture of the small gray shark that fit in the hands of an unknown person.

"A Pondicherry shark? What in the world is *that*?" asked Mr. Savage, our producer, from behind us. I shouldn't have been surprised to see him in the same look I'd always seen him in—aviator sunglasses, a blue button-up shirt, and white pants with fake crocodile-skin shoes. Mr. Savage had come over to the Sacred Sanctuary and Zoological Park, where our family worked when we weren't filming the *Wild Survival!* television series with him, to tell us he had heard from the network what our next animal rescue would focus on. The photo had just come through Mr. Savage's iPad as we sat down to look at the picture.

"It's a shark, duh." Feye, my older brother, laughed. Dad rolled his eyes, once again frowning at Feye's hair. My parents adopted Feye when I was just a baby, so we didn't look like siblings, but we especially didn't look alike now since his naturally dark, wiry hair was currently a bright orange. He was in what my parents called a "neon stage," where all he wanted to wear was brightly colored stuff that stood out against his dark skin and brown eyes. It was driving Dad crazy, but Mom didn't seem to mind so much.

"It's an extremely rare species of requiem shark. There are about sixty species in that family and some of them have even been observed in freshwater," Mom said. "Judging from its size in the picture, this one looks like it could be a juvenile Pondicherry shark."

Her own dark hair was pulled into a ponytail, and her brown eyes were sparkling with excitement. I smiled at her, proud to not only look like her but hopefully grow up to be just like her. I wanted to be a wildlife scientist and work at this zoo full-time, not only help out when I wasn't being homeschooled (we traveled too much to attend regular school).

I know about requiem sharks—they are scientifically known as the Carcharhinidae family. My favorite shark, the tiger shark, is in that family. "If they belong to that family, then they all look like sharks. Not like some shark families that make them look like they are half stingray, half shark," I said.

Feye didn't seem to hear me. Or if he did, he was ignoring me. "Is it called a Pondicherry shark because it is red like a cherry?" he joked. He didn't love sharks as much as I did, so he wasn't the "family expert" on them like I was. Birds? Go to Feye. Sharks? You go to me. I rolled my eyes at him and shook my head. Feye stuck his tongue out at me. Real mature for a fourteen-year-old!

Mr. Savage began to pass out booklets that said "Wild Survival!: Sri Lanka" on the front in big, bold red colors. We receive a booklet before each trip so we know more about where we are going and the different animals we could possibly see. I've collected all my booklets and found them really useful. Sometimes I learn more from the booklets than the books at the library that I go to with my best friend, Alessi. After our last trip to Cuba, we checked out a dozen books on different Caribbean wildlife— our moms caught us staying up way past our bedtime reading and we had to keep the books in the living room.

"I've read a little bit about Pondicherry sharks before. They're gray on top and white below, like many species of sharks. They have black tips on some of their fins, though," I said, blowing a strand of my curly black hair off my face. "They're also known as long-nosed sharks."

"Why is this shark so special if it looks like any other shark?" Feye asked, leaning on his packed backpack and flipping the pages of his booklet quickly. As soon as Mr. Savage told us we had another rescue to film, we all had gone home to pack up our suitcases for the next adventure. I had my pink suitcase next to me, wheels ready for takeoff.

"According to the network, it's one of the twenty-five 'most wanted lost species.' That photo came from Sri Lanka, and it's a pretty big deal if they really have one in an aquarium," Mr. Savage said, his pale hand ruffling his bright red hair.

"Mr. Savage, you said this shark was in an aquarium? Like, a personal one? No way would that be big enough for a shark!"

His blue eyes wandered to our suitcases, making sure we each had a bag, and then he smiled. "We'll see for ourselves. Seems like you're ready to go—grab your bags and *vámonos!*"

Seems like our Spanish was rubbing off on Mr. Savage. We waved goodbye to some employees as we left the lobby of the Sacred Sanctuary and Zoological Park. I texted Alessi that we were off on another adventure, and got a quick smiley response back. Over my shoulder, Feye was taking selfies for his large social media following. "My son the popular influencer," Mom teased, causing Feye to roll his eyes.

"So, what exactly is the plan for filming, Rick?" Dad asked.

"We want to showcase the big, the rare, and the dangerous. We're talking videoing you guys with an angry elephant stampede, the family swimming among the man-eating sharks there, and, of course, releasing this super-rare Pondicherry shark into the wild," Mr. Savage said with theatrical hands. "We heard there are some dangerous sea animals there like sea snakes and jellyfish, too. Up the ante, you know?"

"Um . . ." Mom's voice piped up. "That isn't exactly how we saw the show going."

"Elephants are gentle giants. Sharks are not man-eaters. Sea snakes and jellyfish are fascinating," Dad agreed.

Mr. Savage waved a dismissive hand in the air. "I'm sure we'll capture all that as well! We'll talk more about it when we're there."

With that conversation done, the car started and off we went! On the ride to the airport, I busied myself by texting Alessi more.

ALESSI: Good luck and stay safe!

ADRIANNA: I promise I won't get bitten by a crocodile this time.

ALESSI: Or anything else!

ADRIANNA: Deal, LOL. Guess where we are going.

ALESSI: Um . . . Mexico?

ADRIANNA: I wish—love tacos.

ALESSI: Antarctica?

ADRIANNA: LOL no. Sri Lanka!

ALESSI: Wow! Far away!

I was about to text back when I suddenly heard my brother say, "Earth to Adrianna!" My head snapped up and I saw that the whole family was out of the car, Feye looking at me impatiently.

"Come on, Sis! We're waiting for you!" he said.

Even for it being so late in the day, the airport was crowded, with friends and family exchanging big hugs as they said goodbye or hello for the first time in a while. I always love people watching, and airports are one of the places you can see the best in people.

Once on the plane, I sat down next to the window and let my mind wander back to Alessi's text. "Stay safe," she had said. Our last filming trip was in Cuba, where I got bitten by a crocodile. When Feye and I had saved an injured crocodile's eggs, we came across some dangerous poachers. It had been months since that trip, and my leg had finally healed, with only bright purple scars reminding me of my brush with death. I couldn't stand on my tiptoes for long because it made my leg hurt, but otherwise I was good as new! Well, almost . . .

We hadn't gone on another TV trip since we released the female crocodile mother and half the baby crocodiles back to the wild. The other half of the baby crocodiles went to zoos around the world, to create more babies and help American crocodiles get off the International Union for Conservation of Nature's Vulnerable list. It broke my heart to know they got the label of Vulnerable because humans were wrecking their homes and illegally hunting them and their eggs.

Some turbulence brought my attention back to

the booklet about Sri Lanka opened up on my lap. The country was officially known as the Democratic Socialist Republic of Sri Lanka, and we were traveling to its largest city, Colombo. Sri Lanka was in South Asia, and I realized I knew very little about it. Geography wasn't my strong point. But I knew someone who loved geography—he just happened to be related to me.

"What do you know about where we are going?" I asked my big brother. When he didn't answer, I nudged him with my elbow and realized he had earphones in. He took one out and looked at me.

"Yes?" he asked. I asked my question again.

He shrugged. "Not much. A little bit about the Silk Road, the Buddhist writings about it, and how it was ruled by Britain and known as Ceylon," Feye answered, grabbing a bag of chips from his backpack and taking a few out to eat. He motioned for me to take a few, and I stuck my hand into the salty chips. They were my favorite. I turned back to my booklet and pointed out the title to my mother, who was sitting in the aisle seat in front of me, and asked, "Do they speak English in Sri Lanka, Mom?"

"The official languages are Sinhala and Tamil, but they do speak some English," she answered.

Dad also had turned around from his seat in front of us. "Sri Lanka is home to many cultures, languages, and ethnicities, kids," he chimed in. "The Sinhalese make up most of the population. The Tamils speak Tamil and come from southern India and northeast Sri Lanka. Other religious and ethnic groups in Sri Lanka include Muslims, Burghers, Parsis, and Veddas."

"You've been there before, right, guys?" Feye asked our parents. They nodded.

"You're going to love the food, kids—they are addicted to spices and live to drink tea," Dad said.

I made a show of licking my lips. "I can't wait to

get there." I loved flavorful food full of spices like paprika and cumin and . . . well, I could go on. And tea! I love tea! Peppermint is my absolute favorite tea, but a close second is Ceylon tea, which comes from Sri Lanka.

"It's a beautiful place." Our mother sighed. "Your father got me these *azul* sapphire earrings the last time we were there." Our parents kissed, and Feye and I stuck out our tongues.

"Yuck!" I turned away from my kissing parents and focused on my booklet, jotting down some facts in my trusty field notebook.

Sri Lanka
- *Home to many cultures, languages, religions, and ethnic groups*
- *Spices and teas are popular*
- *Fave sport: cricket*
- *Over 20 species of different whales and dolphins*

I hoped to catch a glimpse of a blue whale while on this trip, as it would be my first time seeing one. Well, one that was alive. We had been to a few museums before where I had gotten to see their bones or pieces of their body, like their heart.

I don't remember when I stopped reading my booklet, let alone fell asleep, but I woke up to light from the open window pouring on my face, my favorite blanket wrapped around my body. It had my favorite animal on it—an echidna! Echidnas sort of look like a mash-up of a ton of animals. They have spines like a porcupine, a snout that looks like a bird's beak, a pouch like a kangaroo's or koala's, and they lay eggs like a lizard. Some people call them spiny anteaters, but I think "echidna" is the perfect name for this little mammal from Australia. My mom had found this blanket when she and Dad were traveling in Australia before they had me.

I sat up to look out the window and saw waters

the most beautiful shade of turquoise that blended into a sandy white beach. Beyond the beach I could see expansive green forests. I grabbed my backpack from under the seat in front of me and rummaged around for my camera. Once I had it out, I took a picture of my first glimpse of what must be Sri Lanka. *Wow. It's gorgeous.*

The flash went off and woke up Feye, who had been sleeping next to me. "Oops, sorry!" I said and looked down at the camera and went to the photo gallery to see my picture. It was all black. *Weird . . .*

I turned the camera over and saw the protective lens cap was still on. *Dang it!*

I held the camera up again and took another picture. "Did it come out this time, or did you forget the camera lens again?" Feye asked, hitting the button that made his chair go from a sleeping position to a sitting position. I held it up for him to see and said, "I always do that! I've just got to get used to it, is all."

"That was really nice of *Abuela* to give you a camera for our next adventure," Feye commented. I nodded. Our grandmother was the best! She had heard me going on and on for months about wanting a camera after our family went to a photography exhibition about the behind-the-scenes fishing industry. Inspired to make a difference, I was determined to start getting out there and taking photos of lots of wildlife I ran into!

As the plane got closer to the land, our captain told us to fasten our seat belts, so I buckled up and put away my camera and booklet. I would just have to read about the Pondicherry shark when we got to where we were staying!

CHAPTER TWO

*"A*yubowan! Welcome to Colombo, Villalobos family! We are very excited to show you around our beautiful Sri Lanka," boomed a man with midnight-black hair and brown skin. His dark eyes twinkled with warmth, and he gave me a strong handshake that made my bones feel like they were rattling inside me. Still, I liked the big smile he gave me, and I couldn't help but notice the large gap between his pearly white teeth.

Mr. Savage and the camera crew—made up of Mark, Alice, and Connor—had left us with instructions at baggage claim to find a man carrying a small whiteboard with our name on it. They were going to drop off all the luggage at the hotel where we would be staying while we went on a small island tour.

"My name is Manil, and I'll be taking care of you. This is my boy, Zev. When I told him I would be giving the *Wild Survival!* family a tour of our island, he just insisted he come with me. He's been a fan of your YouTube channel for a while, and ever since your crocodile episode aired, I think we've seen it a hundred times now. I hope you don't mind."

Our mother shook her head. "Not at all! I'm sure Adrianna and Feye would love to have another kid around. It's very nice to meet you, Zev. What a lovely name."

Zev smiled broadly. He looked exactly like his dad, except without the wrinkles. "*Ayubowan!* Hello! And thank you! It is very nice to meet you, too, Mrs. Villalobos. My name means 'wolf.'"

I gasped. "Our last name means 'wolf,' too! 'Lobo' is Spanish for wolf, and 'lobos' is plural, so that means more than one wolf," I excitedly proclaimed. I was proud of knowing two languages and liked teaching people Spanish words.

"Cool! What does 'villa' mean, then?" Zev asked.

"Nothing cool. It means village," Feye interrupted, picking up his bag and joining the adults, who were walking ahead and toward Mr. Manil's car. Zev and I ran after them, helped put the bags in the back of the car, and piled in. Us kids were in the back while all the adults sat up front.

Zev was telling Feye and me about the stuff we were seeing outside the window when I heard Mr. Manil say, "It will be interesting to see if the shark really is the rare Pondicherry shark."

I whipped out my field notebook and pencil and started writing as Mr. Manil talked about the Pondicherry shark. I always wrote in this notebook about the different animals we got to work with. The last one had been the American crocodile!

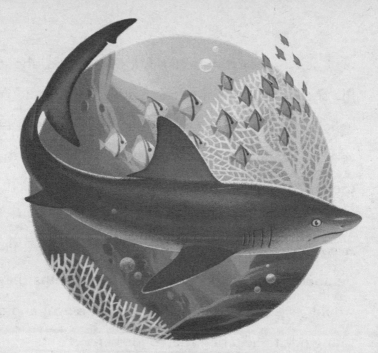

PONDICHERRY SHARK

- These sharks are gray on top and white on the bottom.

- They can grow up to 3.3 feet (1 meter) long.

- Although seldom sighted in recent decades, their habitat was known to be the coastal waters of the Indo-Pacific Ocean region.

- Pondicherry sharks are a critically endangered, very rare species.

I felt a little bit better knowing more about the shark we were going to possibly see. I couldn't believe nobody had seen these sharks in almost fifty years . . . could they really be extinct? That meant there were no more of them around on our planet!

Maybe they were just really good at hiding? According to Mr. Manil, scientists knew very little about these sharks and every few months they would get a few people asking to rent a boat and a tour guide to help find the Pondicherry shark.

"They're known as 'lost sharks,'" said Zev, and I scrunched up my nose. Lost sharks?

"But we know they're around here somewhere. So, are they really lost?" I asked, and Feye let out a snorty giggle. I ignored him.

Mr. Manil also laughed but explained, "No, Adrianna. They're called the 'lost sharks' because scientists know so little about them. When they go looking for these lost sharks, sometimes they find new species that science didn't know about before. There are some really famous people who study these lost sharks. It's important work!"

I wrote that down in my notebook.

"How many sharks are there in the world, Dad?" Zev asked, and I looked up from my notebook. Mom had turned around to answer when I said, "We keep finding new species, so it is hard to keep track of the exact number! But it's over five hundred shark species right now."

Mom winked at me, proud. I winked back. "Wow! That's a lot more than I thought!" Zev exclaimed.

"Adrianna, do you know how many species of shark have been found around Sri Lanka?" my dad asked. I thought about it. If there were over five hundred species of sharks and Sri Lanka was surrounded by water . . .

"Over three hundred species!" I said proudly, confident I was correct.

Feye shook his head, a smile on his face. "Give or take about sixty species," he said. Dad nodded and extended a hand to give him a fist bump. It's a thing they've done ever since they watched some Disney movie about a robot who likes giving out fist bumps in a funny way.

"Showed up the Mother of Sharks," Dad said. He had given me that nickname when I was younger since I loved working with the aquarists at the Sacred Sanctuary and Zoological Park to help hatch baby sharks from their egg cases. I loved seeing them wiggle around in the cases before they were ready to be born.

That still seemed like a lot of shark species, even if sixty was only a small bit of the over five hundred species. "Someone read the Sri Lanka booklet Mr. Savage gave us!" Mom said, coming to my defense.

"Do you know that sharks have relatives?" Mr. Manil said. "Kind of like your cousins, they also have cousins. They are the stingrays; the skates, which are like another type of stingray; and chi-maeras." I thought of our cousins back at home, like Emmanuel and Nuni.

"Mom, isn't a chimaera a mythological creature?" Feye asked, now really interested in the conversation. Mythology? Like the Athena play I was in for all the homeschooled kids a few years ago?

Mom shook her head. "No, that is chimera. C-H-I-M-E-R-A. This is chimaera, C-H-I-M-A-E-R-A. The first one, yes, is a mythological creature. A really scary beast made of a bunch of animal parts like a lion's head, wings of an eagle, and a snake for a tail." I could not imagine that would be a nice-looking animal.

Mom continued, explaining, "The second one is a real animal. They're actually even more distant cousins than the stingrays and skates! They usually live in really deep waters."

CHIMAERA

- These unique-looking fish live in all the world's oceans except for the Antarctic.

- Unlike sharks that have rows of teeth, all chimaeras have tooth-plates to eat a variety of prey.

- They are most closely related to sharks and rays.

- Chimaeras typically inhabit deep water and have been found as far down as 8,500 feet (2,600 meters).

"There are a lot of species of rays, skates, and chimaeras in the world. In total with sharks, there are over one thousand species!" said Dad.

Now THAT was a lot.

"Is the Pondicherry shark only found in Sri Lanka?" Feye asked.

"Nobody really knows, *mijo*," Dad answered. "That's why it's so important we save this shark. It could be the very last of its species."

"Where is this shark?" I asked, looking out the window.

"Coming up! It's apparently being held in an at-home aquarium," Dad said.

I got real sad at that thought as Mr. Manil parked the car in front of a small, bright pink building. The roof was made of orange curved tiles and the white windows were wide open. Music, laughter, and people chatting could be heard even through the closed car doors. We undid our seat belts and stepped outside the car.

Could it really be the last one of its kind? Well, maybe it was living a good life in the aquarium—it was dangerous out there in the wild!

CHAPTER THREE

As we opened the glass door, a little bell jingled. This building wasn't a house at all—it was a restaurant. An older lady, who looked just as old as our *abuela*, came out and greeted us with a toothy grin. She wore a bright orange skirt that had yellow flowers on it that matched the yellow shirt she was wearing. I wanted to tell her how pretty her red lipstick was, but before I could say anything, she spoke.

"Come, come, sit," she said in English and picked up some menus to hand to us. Mr. Manil said something in a different language—I would have to ask him to teach me some. She again smiled and pointed to the back of the restaurant. There was a slight breeze and I looked up to see a few ceiling fans that provided the background ambience of a soft whirring noise.

"Yes, come see the shark," she said and led us back, stopping by a table near the aquarium. If I had thought this shark was living a good life in an aquarium, I was very wrong. It didn't look like any of the aquariums I had seen! The aquariums at the zoo, and even some in the homes of Mom and Dad's friends, had colorful rocks on the bottom and included live plants or coral. I remember one aquarium even had a small castle for Nemo the clown fish to swim in and out of.

But there were no colorful rocks or coral or plants in this aquarium. There was no castle and no other fish in the tank. It was only a few feet long, which was bigger than most home fish tanks, but not big enough for even a small shark like this. This gray shark, about eighteen inches long, could swim from one side of the tank to the other in a few seconds, and then it would turn around and do it all over again. The shark was all alone with some bubbles. It looked like it had a sad frown on its face . . . but all sharks sort of look like that, I guess.

Another family was eating their food near the aquarium. The smallest of the kids stood up on his chair and started banging his hand on the glass whenever the shark swam by.

Thwack-thwack-thwack!

"Hey! Please stop that!" I said as we went past. I sat down with the rest of our group. Their family stopped eating and looked at me.

"It isn't nice," I explained. "It scares the shark because they can hear the noise inside the aquarium. Please don't do it." The kid looked at me for a few seconds and then saw the shark coming back to his end of the tank. Once again, he smacked the glass.

"Stop! Please! You're scaring it!" I said, a little louder.

"Adrianna. We do not yell in a restaurant," Dad said, and Feye grabbed my wrist. Zev looked uncomfortably between me and the kid's family. The kid kept hitting the glass. *Thwack-thwack-thwack!* I looked at my parents and Feye—why weren't they saying anything?

It's as if Zev could read my mind. "They probably don't know what you are saying, Adrianna. Remember, English isn't a language everyone in every country knows how to speak."

Of course! How could I forget that? I looked at Mr. Manil and said, "Mr. Manil, can you please tell them what I said? About the noise scaring the shark? Please?"

He nodded and walked over to the family. I couldn't hear what he was saying to them, but the family stopped eating again to nod at Mr. Manil and he gave me a thumbs-up.

Thwack-thwa—

I turned my head around and saw the dad holding the young child's hand and pulling him down so he was sitting again. You didn't need to understand a language to see he was getting in trouble with his dad. I didn't mean to get him in trouble . . . I just didn't want the shark to be scared.

My eyes scanned the menu, seeing a fish emoji alongside many of the menu items. I wondered if any of the fish were caught illegally. We took forever to order the food, and when it finally came, I almost forgot about the shark swimming next to me in a too-tiny and too-plain aquarium. Almost. We all must have been starving because we ate in silence, the only noise from our table being the slurps and contented sighs from our mouths as we devoured our food. Zev spooned some of his vegetarian kottu onto my plate when he saw me eyeing it. I smiled. Between mouthfuls I looked up to see rice and curry on everyone's table, with various kinds of bread piled high in the middle of each family. I grabbed from the pile of our roti-style flatbreads and dunked a piece into my dhal curry.

I had never tasted food that exploded with such flavor, and my mouth began to water all over again as I spied fried snacks leaving the kitchen and being placed on other tables. After our meal, my mother asked Mr. Manil to translate for the shop owners, Mr. and Mrs. Gamage, that we wanted to talk to them about the shark.

"Can you please tell Mrs. Gamage that this could possibly be a Pondicherry shark, a very rare species here? It could be the last of its kind and we would love to take a fin clip sample to test and see if it is indeed one," Mom said.

I looked at her. *How were we going to do that?!*

A fin clip meant my parents wanted to do a genetic analysis on the shark to identify if it was a

Pondicherry shark or not. And that made sense—it was one of the most accurate ways to identify a species. My parents would take a small clip (so small the shark wouldn't feel a thing!) from the fin. It would be placed in a tube filled with the chemical ethanol to keep it preserved until the DNA test could be run. I wasn't confused about that . . . but I was confused about how we would test the tissue sample.

Feye saw the uncertainty on my face. "Mom and Dad have a marine biologist friend here that they are going to meet up with."

"How do you know that?" I asked.

"I overheard them talking to her. She's got a whole operation here," he answered. I nodded. Guess I would meet her soon enough.

Mr. Manil translated what my mom had said. The owners nodded their heads, and Mr. Gamage eventually said something back. It wasn't until then that I realized how hot it was in here, seeing the sweat on Mr. Gamage's upper lip. He wore a plain cream-colored shirt that was stained with sweat, now matching our own sweaty clothes. "They said yes," Mr. Manil said, "but to please be careful, as many customers come here to see the shark. They don't want it hurt too badly—it must look pretty."

"If it is a Pondicherry shark, it should be in the wild," Feye mumbled under his breath.

If this were the last one—EVER—shouldn't it be in a nicer aquarium where it could be protected? Where scientists could learn more about it?

Before I could say anything to my parents, *thwack-thwack-thwack!*

The kid was back hitting the tank. Why weren't the parents doing anything about it? Before my mother or father could reply to what the owners had said, I stood up quickly.

Zev, who was next to me, tugged at my shirt. He was trying to get me to sit back down.

"You're stressing the shark out!" I hadn't meant to yell, but it came out louder than I had intended. My mother gave me *the look*. I knew I was in trouble. I wondered if Mr. Manil was going to translate what I had said, but Zev must have done it for me. Maybe he was saying sorry for me, too?

The small child was once again being chastised by his own parents while Zev said something to the Gamages.

"I'm sorry," I squeaked.

Before the Gamages could reply, my mother said, "Mr. Manil, please give Mr. and Mrs. Gamage our sincerest apologies for the outburst my daughter just had. She knows better than to yell." As Mr. Manil translated, Mom stood up and motioned with her finger for me to follow her.

I picked up my chair and pushed it under the table. I bowed my head down and said, "I am very sorry for yelling. I didn't mean to. Please forgive me." Then I followed my mom to the front door of the restaurant, where she was waiting for me.

"Adrianna Villalobos, you know very well that your father and I did not raise you to yell when you do not get your way. That is *not* how you have a conversation with someone," she said, her eyes stormy.

"Mom, they can't do this! Look at the shark; it's clearly suffering. They probably have kids hitting that glass every day, and that poor shark hears it all and it can't go anywhere to get away from the loud noise!"

Mom was not impressed with my explanation. "I will agree with you that any shark, regardless of the species, deserves a better habitat than where this one is right now. But there's a lot to consider with this specific situation. Unfortunately, this isn't something we can just change on the spot," she said. She bent down to look me in the eyes. "You will not always get what you want. We will not always be able to save every animal, even if we really want to. You are a brilliant kid, Adrianna. But I want you to know that yelling at someone because they disagree will not get you anywhere. Saying your side louder will not make them want to listen to you."

I hung my head low. She was right. "I'm sorry, Mom."

"I know, *mija*. I'm glad you apologized to them . . . but I'm very disappointed by your behavior. I think you, your brother, and Zev should go outside. Maybe Zev can show you guys around the area while Dad and I get the fin clip."

She told me to stay where I was and I felt my cheeks get hot. I didn't want to cry, especially not in this restaurant in front of a bunch of strangers. I watched Feye and Zev leave the table and walk toward me.

Feye took my hand and said, "Let's go," before Zev opened the door. The little bell once again jingled, and we walked out without looking at anyone else.

CHAPTER FOUR

I held open the old glass door and jumped down a pair of steps in one high jump. As my sandals hit the dirt sidewalk, I kicked at a rock and yelled out, "Ugh!" I wondered if I had to put a *moneda* in the jar for that one . . . it wasn't technically a bad word.

How could they keep a beautiful shark in a small tank like that?! Didn't they know how important sharks were to the oceans?!

Feye put a hand on my shoulder as I crossed my arms and turned away from him and Zev.

"Adrianna, you need to chill," Feye said in a low voice. He used that voice with me whenever he was trying to calm me down. I puffed out a dramatic sigh and looked past him and at Zev.

"Why didn't the parents understand that what the kid was doing was wrong?" I said. We sat on the dusty steps and I tucked my legs under my long blue skirt. It was one of my favorites and I was glad I'd packed it into my suitcase.

"Well, thanks to movies and the news, a lot of people think sharks are these fearsome monsters that eat everything—including people. So many people don't care for sharks. They have that 'the only good shark is a dead shark' mindset." Zev shrugged.

I didn't have any reply. He was right. People back home feared sharks for the same reason.

"So what would you like to see?" Zev asked, changing the subject. "We can go wherever you want."

I couldn't tell if it was hotter inside or outside the restaurant. Or maybe it was my face, red with embarrassment from being scolded by my mom in front of so many people.

"We should stay close to the restaurant, like our mom said," Feye commented, wiping sweat off his forehead.

"Or we can have Zev take us somewhere cool," I suggested, my hands gesturing to our new friend and the awesome adventures he could take us on.

"There is a neat water hole nearby. Lots of kids hang out there, and sometimes there are even elephants!"

"We could talk to other kids about the Pondicherry shark!" I said excitedly. If adults wouldn't listen, maybe some kids my age would understand.

"Or we could stay close to the restaurant," Feye repeated. I let out a huff of air.

"It isn't too far. Like a ten-minute walk." Zev shrugged, his hand reaching up to scratch his shaggy hair.

"I say we go! I want to see some elephants!" I squealed.

Elephants! These would be Sri Lankan elephants, which are a subspecies of the Asian elephant and native to Sri Lanka. I remember reading in our booklet that they were listed as Endangered by the IUCN, which stands for the International Union for Conservation of Nature. Our parents had explained to us that the IUCN was the world's oldest environmental organization in the world. Their job is to tell scientists and conservationists, like our parents, how animals and plants are doing.

"Endangered" meant the Sri Lankan elephants were in danger of becoming extinct. I didn't know why, though, and wanted to ask Zev if he knew.

"Well, I'm staying here," Feye said, leaning against the outside wall of the restaurant.

"But, Feye, it could be a 'Feye and Adrianna Mission'!" I pouted.

"It isn't a 'Feye and Adrianna Mission' when it isn't just us two. Go ahead . . . I don't want to get in trouble," Feye muttered, and with that he fished his headphones out of his pocket and plugged them into his phone. Before I could protest, I could hear his loud music pumping out of the headphones.

Fine. He didn't want to come? It would be an "Adrianna and Zev Adventure," then.

"Come on, Zev," I said, grabbing his arm. "Lead the way to the elephants!"

We turned away from the restaurant and toward the busy street. Zev held my hand tightly as we weaved between the bicycles, motorbikes, cars, and people that filled the streets. I couldn't tell where the actual street stopped and the sidewalk began.

"Zev, why are the Sri Lankan elephants endangered?" I asked. A car honked its horn at the same time, so I had to yell my question again to make sure he had heard.

"Hunting is a big reason. Some did it for pleasure. But some people killed the elephants because they were seen as pests by farmers. The elephants would come onto their land to eat and drink water. It's a shame because they are so important to Sri Lankan culture."

"How so?" I asked.

"Well, they are all over our art, for one!" Zev said and stopped walking to point at the mural next to us. Sure enough, there was an elephant in the middle of the kaleidoscope of colors. It was a dark gray color and had a headpiece of gold and jade that seemed so lifelike I had to look closely to see it wasn't the real thing embedded into the building. Having taken my backpack with me out of the car and into the restaurant, I reached around to grab my camera and snap a photo.

Click!

"Look around, you'll see them everywhere," Zev

continued, and I whirled in a circle to really study my surroundings. I had been so busy dodging people and vehicles, I hadn't taken a second to look at the stone and wooden carvings dotted along the pathways and on the sides of buildings. All around me were elephants with beautiful ornamentations on their heads and draped on their large backs. I let out a "Wow" under my breath. The details were absolutely stunning!

Click! Click! Click!

"But they are protected under Sri Lankan law. Catching or killing a wild elephant carries a fine, and taking the life of an elephant is illegal under any circumstances," Zev explained.

"Well, that's good to hear!" I said as Zev once again grabbed my hand and pulled me along toward a main road that looked like the ones at home except that it had dense forest on each side. I was so entranced by the different greens of the forest that I didn't realize Zev had stopped walking, which led to me running into his back.

"Why did we stop?" I asked.

Zev pointed ahead to one side of the dense forest, where leaves from the tall trees were shaking. He mumbled something that sounded like "*aliya,*" but before I could ask what he said, a large dark figure emerged. It was an elephant! It was huge, and I noticed lighter patches on its ears, trunk, and belly. I had never seen a wild elephant and didn't quite know what to look at first. Its gleaming white ivory tusks? Its long trunk that was tentatively sniffing the air? The wide column-like legs? The long, flat ears that twitched with every noise as traffic slowed to a stop to stare?

"Is it the head female?" I asked. I didn't know much about elephants, but I knew that females were in charge of elephant herds.

Zev shook his head. "No. It's a male. But the female must not be too far behind."

It was like she was listening. Suddenly, a bigger elephant appeared from the dense forest. It looked exactly like the first one, but this one had no tusks. She made a noise with her long trunk and then ambled out into the middle of the road with her large feet. Her tail whipping from side to side, she examined each vehicle and person that had stopped to let her through. More rustling from the forest took my attention away from her and the smaller male to see other elephants making their way out into the road.

Elephants of every size came out! Some were three times our size, and a few smaller ones followed close behind. I lost count of how many there were. But I did notice that almost every single one didn't have tusks.

"Zev, are these all females? They don't have tusks!" I asked.

"Some are. Some are baby elephants," he said.

He then started whispering facts about Sri Lankan elephants, making sure not to make too much noise to attract any attention from them. I whipped out my notebook and furiously wrote down everything Zev was telling me as we watched the beautiful animals slowly cross the road.

I stopped writing as an elephant lifted its trunk high in the air and let out a trumpet, and I wished I hadn't left my camera in my backpack. It was another male, this one with large pink markings on both of his ears. He was the last one of the group and was wildly swinging his trunk from side to side as if telling everyone to back off and let him through. As he disappeared into the dense green leaves on the other side of the road, the traffic on the main road started up again and it was like nothing had ever happened.

"Well, we know where to go now!" Zev laughed as we hurried after the elephant herd. Zev reassured

SRI LANKAN ELEPHANT

- This is the largest of the four subspecies of Asian elephants.

- They are considered an endangered species. There's thought to be fewer than four thousand left in the world.

- Herd sizes usually range from twelve to twenty individuals but can be larger.

- These herds are led by the oldest female elephant (known as the matriarch).

me we were close to the water hole, and after a few minutes of walking in silence, whacking away thick leaves from our faces, we made it! But the elephants were nowhere in sight.

"Maybe they weren't thirsty. They might come back," Zev offered. I nodded and looked at the water hole, which was full of local children. Some were swimming in the dark water, and I shuddered. While I wasn't afraid of crocodiles after I had been bitten by one in Cuba, I still wasn't the biggest fan of murky water I couldn't see through. I would not be swimming in this.

"Zev! *Ayubowan!*" we heard a voice call out, and I saw Zev wave to a small group of kids our age, who then made their way to where we were. The two girls were wearing matching yellow dresses with black-blue-and-white beading around the collars and hems. The beading was fashioned to look like flowers, which matched the beads in their long, curly black hair. One girl had her hair in pigtails, and the other had a ponytail. The guy wore a dark blue shirt with black pants. Their bare feet were covered in mud.

"This is Manisha, Punya, and Dilip. We go to school together!" Zev explained.

I waved and smiled as wide as possible. "Hi, I'm Adrianna. Nice to meet you!"

"Oh! You're part of the family Zev was talking about coming to see a rare shark, right?" Manisha asked, tugging at her ponytail with her hand. I couldn't help but notice her bright pink nail polish. I don't get to wear nail polish because it would just flake off while working with animals.

I nodded. "Yeah, that's me! What do you guys know about the Pondicherry shark?" I wanted to know everything they knew—maybe they knew stuff about this shark that wasn't in the booklet Mr. Savage had given us.

Dilip shrugged. "Not much. My dad is a fisherman and he says there are a ton of species like that here in Sri Lanka. He sometimes catches them."

"On purpose?" I asked.

He shook his head. "No, as bycatch. He's targeting other fish, but the sharks like the bait he uses so he catches them instead. I think he throws them back."

"Why would he do that? Sharks are scary!" Punya said, digging her bare toes into the squishy dirt we were standing on.

"Not all sharks are like that," I said. "There are so many different species and most of them don't hurt people. We're not on their menu."

"Their menu?" asked Manisha.

"Yeah, like we aren't what they typically eat. Sharks usually eat ocean animals like fish, seals, dolphins, and turtles," I explained.

"Some even eat other sharks!" Zev added.

The trio of friends scrunched up their noses. Okay, maybe they didn't find that cool . . .

Dilip opened his mouth to say something when a trilling noise came out of his pocket. He held up a finger, as if to say, "Hold on," and looked down at his phone, which said "AMMA" in big capital letters.

"*Amma! Kohomada?*" he asked into the phone.

I looked to Zev, who whispered, "He's asking his mom how she is."

Whatever language Dilip was speaking, it sounded beautiful. It was almost as if he was singing instead of just talking to his mom. With a *beep*, he hung up the phone and looked at us. "That was my mom. She wants me home because it is getting late."

I looked at Zev, who was now looking at his own phone and grimacing. He held the phone up to me, showing we had been out for almost an hour! "Have a nice day, my friends! *Suba davask!* I'll see you at school!" he said and grabbed my hand, leading us back the way we had come.

I waved over my shoulder. "Goodbye! Nice meeting you!" Manisha, Punya, and Dilip waved in return and I saw them heading the other way before we disappeared back into the forest. "We might want to run," Zev suggested, and I nodded. Running wasn't exactly what I wanted to do in a skirt and sandals, but I didn't want to worry our parents since we had been gone for so long.

CHAPTER FIVE

Mom, Dad, and Mr. Manil weren't thrilled we had gone off so far during our Adrianna and Zev Adventure, but they were fascinated to hear we had come across a herd of Sri Lankan elephants. According to Mr. Manil, it was rare to have a herd so close to one of the main cities, and therefore we must be lucky.

Mr. Savage, on the other hand, was stoked. "Wild elephants?! Perfect. We need to film a giant, stampeding herd for part of the episode. Nothing screams danger like a giant bull elephant charging atcha!"

Dad and Mom just rolled their eyes, with Dad joking to Mr. Manil, "Don't pay attention to our overly enthusiastic producer." Mr. Savage didn't even hear the dig, too occupied with recording a voice memo to himself about "violent elephants."

I looked at Feye and asked if they had gotten the fin clip and he nodded, explaining how they had met up with the marine biologist my parents were friends with, and that we would have dinner with her tonight. After some quick hugs and a big thank you, Mr. Manil and Zev dropped us off at the hotel where we would be staying while in Sri Lanka, along with Mr. Savage and the film crew.

Changing into a simple T-shirt and shorts, I was excited to meet this marine biologist friend and learn from her. It didn't take long for dinner to come around and for me to get to do just that.

"Dr. Chandrika! Over here!" my mom said as a woman with beautiful ebony hair came toward us. Her golden dress shimmered in the surrounding candlelight as she weaved between guests and servers.

"Hello again!" She waved enthusiastically and ran into my mom's outstretched arms for a hug. After she gave a kiss on the cheek to my father and nodded toward Feye, her green eyes turned to me, a smile forming on her face.

"And you must be little Adrianna. I've heard so much about you!"

Little?! I was almost all grown-up, thank you very much.

"It's nice to meet you, Dr. Chandrika. I hear you're a marine biologist," I answered as we all sat down to eat.

My dad laughed. "Here we go. Get ready for 'twenty questions about your job' in rapid fire, Dr. Chandrika."

I looked in the direction of my dad, stuck my

tongue out, and then looked back at the scientist at our table. Well, the one I wasn't related to.

"I am a marine biologist! I study blue whales and their movements both here and around the world," she answered, quickly glancing over the menu since she saw a waiter coming in our direction.

While we all decided on food, the table grew quiet. But as soon as the menus were whisked away, I went back to asking Dr. Chandrika about her work.

"So as a marine biologist, do you just basically live on a boat?" I asked.

She shook her head, her golden earrings tinkling together.

"That's a myth! I work behind a desk, too—analyzing all the data I collect out in the field, writing it up, asking for money. I also run the organization Waves of Action, where we do educational marine science outreach in the Sri Lanka community," she said.

"Do you have a fancy building?" Feye asked.

"No, just a regular building." She laughed. "But we host a lot of events there—we're hoping to have a big ocean appreciation event soon! I just came out of a meeting with some local sponsors."

"How'd it go?" Mom asked, taking a sip of her water.

"I think it went okay. I mentioned that we possibly had a rare shark we're doing DNA tests on right now and they were super interested in that. Funny how some people are fascinated by sharks and others think of them as monsters."

"They aren't monsters, though," I mumbled. "I wish they could see that . . ."

Mom said something else, but I didn't listen to a word she said because I could feel an idea blossoming in my head. Thoughts racing, I realized I had the perfect way to celebrate sharks with the people of the Sri Lanka community—a party! Just like Dr. Chandrika said! Who doesn't like parties?

"Adrianna? What is it, *mi tesoro*?" Mom asked, noticing my thinking face.

"*Mami*, I think . . . I just thought of a way to get others to see sharks the way we do." I smiled.

"Well, would you like to fill your mother in on this brilliant idea of yours?" Mom teased, lightly tickling my sides. I giggled and tried to squirm out of her grip, almost jumping out of my seat and in the way of the server who had our food ready.

Once he had put the plates down, I began to explain my idea of a shark party. "I got the inspiration from what Dr. Chandrika said about her ocean appreciation event. What if we hosted our own festival that was all about shark appreciation? There must be some cool shark scientists here. Maybe we can invite them to give a talk or two. And maybe you guys can release the shark in the small tank back into the wild!" I said.

"I bet Mr. Savage would be interested, especially since our original shark rescue plan went down the drain," Feye suggested in between mouthfuls of his highly aromatic food. I would have to remember to steal a bite before he ate it all.

There was silence as the adults looked at me and put their own "thinking faces" on while they ate their food.

"It isn't a bad idea, *mi cariño*," my dad said, turning to my mom.

"It might . . . actually work." Mom nodded. "And we can get Dr. Chandrika involved!"

"I definitely know of a few scientists who would be keen to help out. And we can use my connections with Waves of Action to see what else we can do." She nodded enthusiastically. "I think the locals would be interested—especially if there is food!"

"We'll tell Mr. Savage over breakfast about your plan and see what he and the network think," Dad said, giving me a wink and smile.

The support made me so happy! As my parents and Dr. Chandrika talked more about "the logistics" of my idea (whatever that meant), Feye took a picture of his almost-finished food "for his fans." He has an Instagram where he posts pictures of our travels and our work with animals. *Eye roll.* I picked up my own phone and quickly texted Alessi:

ADRIANNA: Just came up with a good idea for the show and the 'rents are happy about it!

ALESSI: What was the idea???

ADRIANNA: Some locals here seem to be afraid of sharks. So, we are gonna throw a shark appreciation party!

ALESSI: That sounds like your kind of party! But will people come?

That stopped me right in my tracks. It wouldn't

exactly count as a party if it was just our family and the crew. Would anyone show up? Dr. Chandrika seemed to think so, but it's not like we had friends here ... But I knew someone who did! I smiled, remembering my new friend Zev. And maybe Manisha, Punya, and Dilip would like to go, too! But I was getting ahead of myself.

ADRIANNA: Will work on that. First need Mr. Savage to say okay to the idea.

ALESSI: Good luck!

The next morning, I awoke under the softest sheets I have ever felt. I rolled over to see my mom awake on her side of the bed we shared, reading a book about Sri Lankan wildlife.

"¿Mamá?" I asked, whispering. The boys were still asleep, and we could hear their soft snoring.

My mom adjusted her glasses and smiled at me, giving me a kiss on my forehead. "Buenos días, mija. How did you sleep?" she asked.

"Okay. But I couldn't get the shark out of my head," I sighed, fluffing my pillow up to sit next to her and resting my head on her shoulder.

My mother nodded, wrapping an arm around me. "I know, it's tough seeing animals in distress. Not every place will have big, open spaces for the animals they keep."

"But can't we do anything about it?" I asked.

Mom shook her head. "Not always. Remember, even though you love sharks, it doesn't mean everyone else does. Many find them scary—like monsters, even."

"But they aren't!" I said a little too loudly. I thought about my conversation with Dilip about his dad, the fisherman. And Punya's reaction to his dad seeing and handling sharks. Suddenly, I had an idea.

"You guys! Wake up! I just had an idea on how to get people excited about our shark festival—and save the shark!" I exclaimed.

"Adrianna! Let them sleep," Mom chastised me.

"No, no, this is too important. *Hombres* of the Villalobos *familia*! Wake up!" I laughed, jumping on their bed.

"Oh. My. God. Adrianna, get off!" Feye grumbled, sliding farther under the sheets as Dad's eyes popped open at the rude intrusion I was creating.

I ripped the sheets off his side of the bed and kissed his head. "*¡Levántate!* This is important!"

Dad had pulled himself up, so he was sitting like Mom, and rubbed his eyes, looking at the time on the nearby clock. "It better be at five in the morning! What are you doing up so early, A?"

"I couldn't sleep, but that's not the point," I answered, poking my brother's face until an eye flew open.

"I am up. But if you want to keep your finger, you'll stop touching my face or I'll bite it off," Feye growled.

"Mom! Feye threatened bodily violence!" I mock-wailed, and he grabbed me with both of his arms in a big bear hug and tugged me back onto the bed.

"Feye! Adrianna! *¡Basta!* It's too early and we don't want to wake up any of the neighbors—especially the camera crew next door," Mom reprimanded us, pointing to the wall our beds were joined to, on the opposite side of which were Mark, Alice, and Connor sound asleep.

I took a deep breath and told my family about my conversation with Dilip, Manisha, and Punya. "We should involve the fishing community here! The fishers have already been interacting with the sharks, both dead and alive. And they care about the health of the ocean ecosystem since it's important to their livelihood."

"That's something we'll have to talk to Dr. Chandrika about, but I think that's a really good idea to get the community involved, Adrianna," Dad said.

Mom nodded. "Exactly. We want to make sure we get local scientists involved with this and not contribute to parachute science."

"What the heck is that?" Feye asked. "Is it the science of parachutes? That has nothing to do with sharks."

"No, no. It's when researchers come to a place to do research, but they leave without any investment in the community. It basically makes it so that a region is dependent on outsiders to do scientific work, and that makes it hard for local conservation efforts to take off."

"We definitely don't want to do that!" I said. That sounded terrible. "I really want this to be a community thing where we all work together to create this festival and we all learn from it—even us."

My dad smiled at me. "Exactly. Proud of you for thinking that way, Adrianna. Many adult researchers don't even think that way!"

My dad turned around to talk to my mom, so I got my phone out to text Alessi to see how things were at the zoo when I saw Feye grab for his towel and make his way to the bathroom. Oh no! Feye always took forever in the bathroom. He says he needs to "take his time" because "his fans love his look." Whatever that means! But before I could even get two steps toward the bathroom, he was already inside and locking the door.

Sigh. We were going to be here awhile.

CHAPTER SIX

After quickly showering and changing into a plain T-shirt, khaki shorts, and some sandals, I was ready for whatever the day was going to bring.

"Are we going to film elephants today? I know Mr. Savage said something about that?" I asked in the elevator.

"We already found the Pondicherry shark . . . so the show is basically done, right?" Feye joked. I nudged him with my elbow.

"We don't know yet if it's a Pondicherry shark, remember?" I said.

Feye shrugged as we walked out and toward the delicious smell of food.

We met up with the crew in the hotel's restaurant and were soon stuffing our faces with *pani pol*. Also known as Sri Lankan pancakes, they are made from wheat flour, coconut milk, eggs, and turmeric, with fresh-grated coconut, spices, and some cane sugar. According to our waiter, they are best enjoyed with a cup of tea, so all of us had various hot teas, steam wafting up from the cup in mesmerizing tendrils.

"I hope you enjoyed the small tour yesterday, *familia* Villalobos, because today we are leaving the city and will be going to Pigeon Island National Park! You're going snorkeling with some fierce ocean animals!" Mr. Savage announced during breakfast.

I looked down at my outfit and sighed. Well, I wasn't prepared for *that*! I would have to put on a bathing suit. I wondered where I had left my *traje de baño* . . .

"Assuming there will be sharks at this shoot?" our sound producer said in a sleepy Australian accent. Connor was also eating *pani pol*, which might have been the first time I'd seen him eat something else besides toast and Vegemite for breakfast.

"You assume correctly, Connor. We will just be snorkeling, not diving, so no need for the fancy microphone masks," Mr. Savage said before turning to our videographers. "Mark, Alice, please bring the waterproof gear for the cameras." All three nodded, and I noticed they had two mugs each—one for tea and one for coffee. Strong coffee, by the smell of it.

Well, Mr. Savage was getting his "fierce animals" shot, I guess . . .

"The bill, *karaunaākara*," asked Mr. Savage of our waiter when he came by. I recognized the word *karaunaākara*, which meant "please," because Zev had explained what it meant when he said it to a person yesterday. There are two official languages in Sri Lanka: Sinhala and Tamil. *Karauṇaākara* is Sinhalese. I had practiced a few phrases in both languages before we came, but my pronunciations were still a little rocky.

I had no idea where Pigeon Island National Park was. As we made our way back to our rooms, I typed the park into our maps app on my phone to see where we would be going. A notification popped up letting me know I had a text from Alessi.

"Good morning from home! Good luck, luck, luck today with your idea and filming! Please don't get trampled by elephants."

I had told her about my experience with Zev yesterday while I waited for Feye to finishing showering this morning. She was super interested in hearing about the elephants but seemed a bit more interested in Zev himself.

I sent my best friend back a heart emoji and then looked at the map results. Whoa, that was a heck of a drive!

As we walked into our room, I spied my neon pink bathing suit peeking out of my backpack. Grabbing it, I dashed for the bathroom before Feye could get there first.

"Mom? Dad?" I asked from the safety of the locked bathroom, where I quickly tugged off my shirt and shorts.

"Yes, *mija*?" Dad asked.

"Are we driving to this national park? It seems awfully far away," I said.

"No, I think Mr. Savage said we'll be taking a small chartered plane," Mom answered.

"Will we be meeting Mr. Manil and Zev there?" I heard Feye ask. I hoped we would see them. I liked Zev and thought this trip would be a lot more fun with him coming along. I loved making new friends.

Plus, I needed to talk to him about the shark festival!

I didn't hear the answer, though, because Feye pounded on the door and complained, "Come on, Adrianna, you've been taking forever!"

Flinging the door open, I stepped out of my brother's way and practically flew to the other side of the room. I busied myself with packing for the day, shoving the essentials into my backpack: trusty notebook, waterproof pencil, camera, hat, sunscreen, and some sweet-and-sour gummy bears. They were my new favorite snack that I was determined to bring everywhere!

We met Mr. Savage and the crew in the lobby and were guided to a taxi, which then took us past the airport where we had arrived yesterday and to a body of water behind it. I didn't understand why we were going toward water and not the airport until I saw the plane. Even Feye was excited, taking off his sunglasses to explain, "Holy guacamole! YES!" He took a quick selfie as we walked closer to the plane.

The blue-and-white seaplane had animals of all sorts painted on it. Elephants, octopuses, fish, and what looked like a snake . . . or an eel? I couldn't tell. Our pilot stood next to it, facing away away from us and talking on the phone. When he turned around, a big smile broke out on my face.

"*Ayubowan,* Mr. Manil. I didn't know you were a pilot!" I said, practicing my Sri Lankan greeting.

Just then, Zev popped his head out of the plane! My smile got even bigger, which I didn't think was possible. Once all of us were piled into the plane, Zev began to tell us about the national park we would be visiting. "It's one of only two marine national parks in the country! It was first a sanctuary but was changed to a national park in 2003. It's famous for having some of the best coral reefs."

"So why is it called Pigeon Island National Park

and not Coral Reef National Park?" Feye asked.

"It was named after the rock pigeons found there," Mr. Manil answered from the front.

"Is it super remote?" I asked Zev.

He sort of shook his head. "Kind of. It's near a coastal town called Nilaveli. But Nilaveli and the park were affected by the Indian Ocean tsunami in 2004."

I remembered reading about that. There was a 9.1-magnitude quake off the coast of Indonesia, unleashing a massive tsunami across the Indian Ocean. It impacted even Antarctica and North America, and in Sri Lanka many people lost their lives.

I didn't realize it had hit this place, too. I wondered how bad everything would look. Puerto Rico, where our *abuelos* lived, and where we spent every summer, recently got hit by a category 5 hurricane, the strongest hurricane there is. Even though a few years have passed, our family still struggles. A cousin had lost his entire house, and the walls of my *abuelos'* home were crumbling. After the hurricane, they video called us as soon as they had reception. I remember seeing shattered glass everywhere, doors gone, broken wooden boards hanging where windows once were. Seeing their house destroyed felt awful. I wondered if the people here felt the same after the tsunami.

Once we took off, the trip itself didn't take very long. Over the roar of the engines, Zev pointed out the national park below, which was made up of two bright green islands nestled in the calm turquoise waters. The coral habitat here acted like a breeding and feeding ground for over three hundred species of fish that kept the colorful underwater symphony alive. I once read that coral reefs were like the "rain forest" of our oceans because so many animals call them home. Just as sharks are so important for our oceans, so are corals. I smiled at the view before us. Even from here I could see how white and inviting the sand was.

The beautiful landscape grew bigger as we got closer to the earth once again, and I couldn't help but press my face against the window to drink in every detail as it whizzed past us. Everything here was so brightly colored!

My thoughts were interrupted as the seaplane landed with a loud splash. We had arrived! I could hardly contain my excitement as we docked, and I burst out of the plane and into a sprint down the rickety wooden dock.

"Hello, Nilaveli! We're here!" I shouted. I could hear my parents giggle at my enthusiasm. The sun shone brightly, making the surrounding water sparkle as if thousands of shiny diamonds were on its surface. I took my camera out of my knapsack and snapped a photo, almost forgetting to take the lens cap off!

"Adrianna! Come on! We're not there just yet—get into the motorboat," Connor hollered. Out of all the crew, he and I got along the best. We were already friends from working together at home at the zoo, but since our trip to Cuba where I rescued Duke, a dog he ended up adopting, we had become even better friends. He gives me updates about Duke every day, and even sometimes brings him in to work!

I ran back to our group and climbed aboard, ready to have the salty sea spray hit me in the face. I sat up front, my favorite place to be on fast-zipping boats. And boy, was it ever fast! Zev, who sat up front with me, and I were practically soaked by the time our boat stopped over an expansive coral reef area.

"Alright, everyone, welcome to Shark Point Reef. I want you all to suit up for a snorkel! I want to make sure everyone is comfortable with their equipment. Mark, Alice, can you set up your cameras just in case the family sees something cool? Connor, same goes for you," Mr. Savage instructed. He was in full director mode. At least he was out of his usual getup of white pants and a blue shirt and just in shorts and a T-shirt today. To be honest, it was kind of weird seeing him out of his normal attire.

Already wet, I was tempted to dive in with all my clothes still on. But I did the sensible thing and took off the wet garments, Mom taking them and laying them out in the sun to dry while we were underwater. Dad was on sunscreen duty today, making sure to rub some on all of us before we went swimming. As was our tradition, we all gave one another a kiss on the cheek before getting into the water. I cannonballed in, excited to get back into the ocean. Oh, how I missed it!

As soon as I put my head under the lapping waves, I couldn't believe how many different fish there were! Angelfish, parrotfish, eels, wow! I moved my head from side to side to see Mark and Alice swimming not too far behind me, capturing both the fish and me with their large underwater cameras. I tried my best to ignore them because Mr. Savage always told us to "act natural" when being filmed, so I instead dove down a few feet to poke around the coral crevices to see if I could find any cool animals.

"Talk about what you guys see! Let's hear it!" Mr. Savage's voice carried over the water surface. Director mode was definitely ON.

Anemones, small cleaner shrimp, and—oh my gosh!—a neon green eel! I was pointing the eel out to Alice, who was closest to me with her gear, when a figure next to us with no snorkel let out a noisy stream of bubbles and pointed straight ahead of us. Even though the water was super clear, I had no idea how they spotted the huge sea turtle lazily swimming past. It glided by so effortlessly in the turquoise water.

"Tell us about that turtle, Evelyn!" Mr. Savage said, and I heard Mom giving her take to Mark.

I was so distracted by watching her that I hadn't realized someone had come up behind me. A tap on my shoulder made my head jerk around to see who had poked me. Oh, it was Zev! It was hard to see who was who with these masks on. He pointed up and we both surfaced.

"Did you see the turtle?!" Zev asked. "I tried to make noise so everyone could see it."

I spit my snorkel out of my mouth and gave him a big smile. "That was you?! Oh man, it was amazing! So big!" I said, accidentally swallowing some of the salty water. Yuck.

I heard Zev say he couldn't tell if it was a hawksbill, green, or olive ridley turtle, which often visit the area. As he spoke, Alice surfaced and began filming our conversation. But to be honest, I wasn't paying much attention because I was too busy spitting out the icky taste from my mouth. How could Zev swim without a snorkel to help him breathe?

Just as I stopped gagging, another head popped up near us. It was my brother! "Hey, if you guys stopped chatting, you would see the incoming surprise I *know* Adrianna is gonna love," Feye said, pointing down below us and nodding to Alice to follow us. Feye and I put our snorkels back in our mouths. After we all took a deep breath, we followed him and made our way down a few feet below the surface.

When I finally saw the surprise, I practically let out a yelp of happiness. Sharks! Timid and skittish, they stayed far away from us, but I could tell it was one of my favorite species—blacktip reef sharks. As we bobbed at the surface, a small school of them swam ahead of us, all their black-lined tails flicking feverishly from side to side to propel themselves. There were different sizes circling us from a distance, from what looked to be almost as long as Feye to as small as half my size. I was sure we were seeing adults and juveniles, which were warily observing us as they flew through the crystal-clear sapphire water.

"I hear we are seeing bloodthirsty sharks! Adrianna! Tell me more about them to the camera," Mr. Savage commanded. One of the smaller blacktip reef sharks swam in front of my face as he said this, quickly turning away from me when I blew out some air I had been holding in. I sighed, wanting their curious little faces to come closer.

Taking another deep breath, I dove down to point at the sharks in the camera's view and was about to head to the surface when all the blacktip reef sharks began to scatter, zipping through the

BLACKTIP REEF SHARKS

- Named after their black tips, these creatures are a pale grayish-brown color with snowy-white bellies.
- They prefer shallow, clear water. They are one of the shark species that is commonly spotted by snorkelers swimming around tropical coral reefs in the Indian and Pacific Oceans.
- Most blacktip reef sharks grow to no more than 5.2 feet long (1.6 meters).
- Their diet consists mostly of small fish, but they've also been known to eat shrimp, octopus, and squid.

turquoise water. Looking in the direction they had been fleeing from, I glanced behind Alice to see my favorite shark ever—a tiger shark! Someone must have gotten Alice's attention because she whipped herself and her underwater camera around to capture this gorgeous animal.

Powerfully kicking upward to gulp in some air, I dove right back down to see the large shark lazily swim past us. Unlike the nervous blacktip reef sharks, this large shark knew it was the top predator in the water and acted like it. This shark was my favorite because of their striking patterning and unquenchable curiosity—they tend to stick around for a bit to check things out!

"Adrianna, talk about what you just saw!" Mr. Savage reminded me. "Did the shark try to attack you?!" I watched as the protective "eyclid" of the tiger shark, called the nictitating membrane, popped up as it got closer to Alice's and Mark's cameras.

This one looked HUGE, making the camera crew look quite small. Her mouth was slightly open, so we could see her rows of unique, deeply notched teeth.

"We've just had an awesome encounter here in Sri Lanka. A beautiful female tiger shark is swimming with us in this perfect coral reef here. How could I tell it was a female? No claspers!" I said, once at the surface, before Mr. Savage cut me off.

"Feye, explain what claspers are!" Mr. Savage instructed.

Why couldn't *I* talk about a shark's claspers, the bit of outer anatomy on a shark that showed if it was male or female? Sigh.

While my brother talked, I took the opportunity to take a deep breath and dive down to see the sharks again. I watched as the tiger shark slowly moved on from us, no longer interested, until I could barely make out her outline. It felt like a dream! A wild tiger shark in our first underwater adventure!

TIGER SHARK

- These sharks get their name from the stripes on the sides of their bodies.

- Tiger sharks commonly measure ten to fourteen feet (3.25 to 4.25 meters) long.

- Tiger sharks do their hunting solo, and at night. They have the most varied diet of any shark, consuming fish, seals, crustaceans, sea snakes, turtles—even birds!

- Tiger sharks are considered apex predators and are at the top of the food chain.

But my dream burst when I realized I needed to come back up for air. I was no mermaid! Unlike Zev, who was still swimming energetically despite being under for what felt like a really long time. I felt my chest burning from not breathing and took a few powerful kicks before my head was surrounded by air instead of water once again. Gasping, I took my snorkel out and just floated on the surface.

"You okay, Adrianna?" Connor asked from the boat that had been trailing us snorkelers around as we swam. I looked over at him, seeing Alice at the surface as well, handing her heavy camera to the boat crew above as she chatted to Mr. Savage about camera angles.

I gave him the universal "okay" sign that scuba divers give one another when checking in with their buddies.

Zev popped up next to me as I was still taking big breaths, and I also gave him the okay sign. After a few more moments, I could finally speak.

"I don't know how you do it, Zev. Swimming without a snorkel, I mean. You hold your breath for so long!" I said.

"That? It's called free diving. My dad taught me when I was younger," Zev explained.

I had heard of free diving before. You hold your breath for as long as you can until you return to the surface. It takes a lot of skill to be able to do it for long periods of time like Zev seemed able to do. I had heard some people could hold their breath for up to ten minutes!

Feye popped up next to me and that's when I realized I hadn't seen our parents for a while. I had been too busy looking at all the cool marine animals!

"Do you know where Mom and Dad are?" I asked Feye, who shrugged his shoulders and shook his head. He spat out his snorkel and said, "No. I thought they were with you."

As I treaded water, I did a circle to see if I could spot them.

"What's the matter, Adrianna?" Mr. Savage asked, now next to Connor. He must have heard the distress in my voice. He was probably worried I had been bitten by something again!

"I can't see our parents," I told him, continuing to look in the direction we had come from. Mr. Savage and Connor looked out, too, none of us seeing anything but the ocean's surface.

"Okay, kids, time to get out of the water," Mr. Savage said, and we didn't dare disobey this order by the tone of his voice. One by one, Zev, Feye, and I kicked our legs with all our might and were caught by either Alice or Connor as they helped us onto the boat. Once aboard, I took off my flippers and ran to the side of the boat we had just been on to continue to look out. It was only when Feye wrapped me in a towel that I realized I was covered in goose bumps and shivering.

"*¿Mamá? ¿Papi?*" I called out, suddenly spotting three snorkels a distance away. Four? Maybe Mark and Mr. Manil went with my parents, too.

"Connor, can you see if that's them?" I looked up at the Aussie, who lunged across the boat's bow and grabbed some binoculars that seemed to appear as if by magic.

He was quiet for a second, concentrating as he fiddled with the settings to make the image sharper. All you could hear was our ragged breathing and the waves hitting the hull of the boat. Suddenly he pointed in the direction of the snorkels and said, "Yup! That's them! And it looks like something is wrong!"

CHAPTER SEVEN

"It's my fault, really. I should've been paying closer attention to where I was going," Mom said as Mr. Manil rummaged around his bag for a first aid kit. Usually we got treated by Miguel, our medic, but he wasn't arriving until later today due to a storm that had delayed his plane.

Once Connor had spotted Dad's arm waving to the boat—a sign that someone was in trouble in the snorkel/diving world—our boat zoomed over to them. We helped get everyone out of the water as they explained what had happened. It turned out the group had come across a venomous sea snake

YELLOW-BELLIED SEA SNAKE

- These snakes have a distinctive yellow belly, as the name suggests. They live their whole lives in the sea.
- They have the widest known range of any sea snake and can be found in most tropical ocean waters around the world.
- They can swim backward!
- Out in the wild, yellow-bellied sea snakes make fish their primary source of food.

and, as they tried to back up and give it some space, our mom had run right into the tentacles of a milky white jellyfish.

"Is it a dangerous one, Mr. Manil?" Mr. Savage asked as the Sri Lankan took tweezers out of the first aid kit and hovered over Mom's exposed arm where an angry red mark in the shape of a tentacle was forming. He grabbed one end of the nearly invisible tentacle and tugged it off our mom's skin, throwing it overboard.

Mr. Savage looked toward Mark and asked him, "Did you film it? Add it to the list of dangerous animals to showcase this episode, along with those giant elephants and monster sharks." Mark nodded.

"I don't think so," Mr. Manil said, shaking his head at Mr. Savage

"Is it a box jellyfish?" Feye asked, his face getting a little paler. We had some in the aquarium section at the zoo and had heard horror stories about box jellies from our friends in Australia. Like their name suggests, they are box-shaped and although they are not that big, their venom is very potent and can kill people.

"It could be." Mr. Manil shrugged. "But the box jellyfish in Sri Lanka don't cause many problems."

"Let me see the footage," Mr. Savage asked Mark.

"How does the pain feel, *Mami*?" I asked her.

She winced a bit as she tried to smile at me. "I'm okay, baby. Feels like any other jellyfish sting. You should know how that is!"

I stuck my tongue out at her, remembering the time I dove face-first into jellyfish tentacles while snorkeling in the Galápagos Islands off Ecuador years ago. *Ouch!*

"Some ice and medicine for the pain should make it hurt not so much. But you're a tough woman. I think you'll be okay," Mr. Manil said. We all let out a breath of air we didn't know we had been holding.

"At least this snorkel wasn't for nothing! I did get some cool footage of that sea snake," Mark joked as we all laughed.

"I think we've had enough adventure for a day. We should get back and give the matriarch of the Villalobos family some rest," Mr. Savage concluded. With that declaration, the boat was turned around and headed back to the dock.

This time, I didn't sit up front with Zev. Instead, I carefully walked back to where my parents and Mr. Savage sat, wanting to know if we could talk about the shark festival *now* since we hadn't this morning over breakfast.

Mom had a cup of something warm in her hands while she rested her head on Dad's chest. He continued to hold an ice pack on her arm.

"Mr. Savage, have my parents told you about the idea Dr. Chandrika and I had for the show?" I asked.

"An idea, huh? No, I think we were a little bit

distracted!" Mr. Savage chuckled, pointing to Mom's arm. "You Villalobos gals are going to make me go gray!"

It was meant to be a joke, I think, but I didn't find it that funny. Still, I laughed because I wanted Mr. Savage to be in a good mood when I told him my plan.

"Adrianna, since you helped come up with the idea, why don't you tell Mr. Savage?" my mom said.

I sat down next to my parents and faced Mr. Savage, the fast momentum of the boat making it hard to stand and talk at the same time. Over the roar of the boat engine, I could hear Feye complaining about how he couldn't get a "good shot" of our surroundings. Each time he tried to focus, the boat would jerk and cause his photo to come out blurry.

"Well, after my . . . outburst . . . the other day, I got to thinking about how not everyone likes sharks," I said.

"This is true," Mr. Savage said, nodding.

"Well, what if we show people who might be scared of them how amazing they really are?" I offered.

"How so?" Mr. Savage asked.

"By throwing a shark party! Dr. Chandrika and I were talking about her important outreach work through Waves of Action, and we thought we could throw a Shark Appreciation Festival. We could talk about the different sharks found in Sri Lanka, why they are important, and why people shouldn't see them as these mindless killers," I said. "We could bring in Sri Lankan scientists to do talks, and maybe one of us could do a small talk as well. And maybe, just maybe, we could get that Pondicherry shark freed back into the wild! You could film it all!"

Mr. Savage was quiet as he thought the idea through.

"The network might like the idea of changing

human wildlife relationships through a younger member of our *familia*," Dad suggested.

"True. And it's not something I've seen on the network before . . ." Mr. Savage said, lost in thought.

He clapped his hands together after a few more seconds of silence, his eyes sweeping over us. We all heard Feye say, "Oh come on!" as the front of the boat inevitably got soaked.

"I will speak to the guys tonight and see what they say, but I have a good feeling about this," he said. "You came up with this?"

I nodded and he winked at me. "Good job, Adrianna. Thinking like a producer!"

"More like thinking like a wildlife educator," I said proudly. Mom smiled at me once again. Mr. Savage didn't say anything. He gave me a tight smile and got up to talk to the camera crew about something.

"Do you think he really liked the idea?" I asked my parents.

They nodded. "But it's not just up to him. It's up to the network . . . but here is hoping they like it, too."

With that, I got up and left my parents alone because Mom looked a bit tired. I should know— getting stung by a jellyfish stinks! I made my way up to the front of the boat to join my brother and Zev, who was laughing at Feye's attempts to frantically snap the "perfect shot" for his Instagram grid.

"Hey, Zev! I wanna run an idea by you," I called out.

"Run the idea by me, then, Adrianna," he said, turning his attention from my brother to me and giving me a wide smile.

For the third time that day, I explained the idea about the Shark Appreciation Festival, asking him if he thought anyone would come. As the boat docked and we climbed off and all got into the seaplane waiting for us, he thought about his answer.

"Maybe. Sri Lankans are like everybody else—we

love a good party!" Zev finally answered, speaking loudly since the plane's engine was revving up to get us airborne.

"Think you could invite some of your friends to come? And they could invite some of theirs?" I asked.

He grinned. "Is this a mission?"

I nodded. "A life-or-death mission for that poor shark, Zev. It deserves freedom, but even if we could get it into a bigger tank, that would be a good start."

Zev looked out the window as we flew high above the clouds and lost sight of the shimmery blue water and striking green mountains. "I'll help you out as much as I can."

"Well . . . then I have one more thing you can help me out with," I said and leaned over to tell him my *other* plan.

CHAPTER EIGHT

"Of course, Adrianna Villalobos wouldn't be happy with just throwing a party," Zev said, shaking his head as we walked toward our destination. It was about an hour after we had been dropped back off at our hotel so my mom could rest. While our dad stayed to check up on Mom, Feye and I decided to check out the hotel's pool with Zev, who had gotten permission from his dad to stay with us.

Except, we weren't at the pool. Well, not anymore at least. We had gone down with Feye, who began swimming laps, and I decided we should ditch my brother to go where we were currently headed: the fish market. With the camera from *mi abuela* in my backpack, I had asked Zev to bring me to the fish market so I could take pictures of the sharks there. I was sure that if I could showcase pictures of living Sri Lankan sharks in their natural environment looking beautiful and majestic, and then show them the sad-looking dead ones, then people might not be so afraid of them.

I wouldn't be able to take any pictures of the living sharks all by myself—I wanted to see if Mark and Alice could help me with that part. Hopefully by showing people the contrast between lifeless sharks in the market and vibrant sharks out in the wild, we could inspire people to rethink how they see sharks, make different seafood choices, and not choose shark products.

"Think of it as an undercover mission! Just you, me, and—" I started.

"Don't forget us!" a familiar voice said behind

us. I stopped in my tracks on the sidewalk, turned around, and saw the smiling faces of my new friends Manisha, Punya, and Dilip.

"You have to admit it's better to carry out an undercover mission with friends," Manisha laughed.

"How did you know about this?" I asked, hugging them all.

"Zev called us and told us to meet him at the market with our cameras. We like your idea!" Dilip said, and each one held a camera in their hand.

I turned around to give Zev a big hug and whispered, "Thank you," in his ear.

"Ooooh!" teased Punya, with Manisha and Dilip laughing as Zev and I jumped apart.

I looked back to my new friends and we all continued to walk to the market, Zev leading the way. "So, you know the mission, then? Find sharks and take photos of them," I explained. "Multiple photos of different angles. Make it all artsy."

Manisha pulled out her phone. "Like this?" she asked and shared an image of a great white shark breaching out of the water. I had to hold in a giggle.

"No, not all sharks look quite as dramatic as a great white. I'll point some out when we get to the market!"

It turns out the hotel we were staying at wasn't too far away from the fish market. People filled every available space to look at the catches of the day. As they shouted over one another for prices and haggled to get the best deal, the five of us peeked between arms and bodies to see what lay gleaming on the tables. Some fish were kept whole, their dead eyes staring back at us. Others already had their heads hacked off and lay in buckets as fillets or were set out to dry. Many of these fish had signs with numbers on them and descriptions of what they were. Zev translated as we went around.

We made our way silently through the packed

aisles, listening to the rhythm of the market: the thud of knives cutting up fish, people loudly trying to sell their catches of the day, and the briny smell of fresh fish.

After what felt like forever, we made it out the other side of the market and onto a beach. Dilip made a show of taking in a big breath of fresh air.

"Those long sacks are made out of *kohu lanu*, or coconut fiber," explained Zev as I eyed the rolled-out sacks atop the beach sand with more fish on top, drying in the Sri Lankan sun. Seemingly thousands of tiny sardines and other small fish lay baking under the warming rays. I spotted some big fish chopped into pieces, and hundreds of squid tied up in a bunch together being rotated by some of the fishers.

"How are we supposed to spot any sharks from all these fish, Adrianna?" Punya asked.

"Punya is right—they all look the same to me!" Dilip said.

"Look for the big fish with the fins?" Zev offered.

"They all have fins!" Manisha exclaimed, and we all laughed.

My eyes scanned the mats along the beach and I squatted down, took the protective lens off my camera, and snapped a photo. "Well, why not take a picture of everything we see and then look through them when we get back to the hotel?" I said. They all seemed to think that was a good idea because with a nod, each person went to a different part of the beach to take photos.

As I walked down to a nearby mat where two men were yelling prices, I took a picture of their catches. Moments later, they yelled and shooed me away. I hadn't realized that maybe some of the fishers wouldn't be happy with a tourist taking photos of their catches. I thought about Mom talking about parachute science, and was suddenly worried I was being rude. I hadn't asked before getting in their space.

I scurried away from the angry men and went to a mat a few aisles down. I said hello in Sinhala and held up my camera to mimic taking a photo, to see if the owners of this mat understood I was asking their permission. They smiled and nodded. Once I snapped the photo, I said "thank you" in my very limited Sinhala.

Their mat, along with the dozens in this aisle, was full of a variety of sea creatures. Alongside the crabs, squid, and barracudas I could make out were dozens of other animals I didn't recognize. But then there was one I very much did. The owners—women sitting on small plastic stools—watched me as I focused on the peculiar-looking sharks.

"I found her!" I heard Zev say as I continued to snap photos of the four different shark species in front of me.

"What is *that one*?" Dilip said.

"Hammerhead shark," I explained. I stood up

and bowed my head in thanks to the women, once again practicing my Sinhala for "thank you."

Punya clapped. "Your pronunciation's getting better!"

"Are they called hammerhead sharks because their heads look like a hammer?" asked Dilip, wanting to know more. I nodded and took off my backpack, rummaging around for my field notebook, where I had written about these species. Finally finding it, I flipped to the sharks page and shared it with the gang while Zev read it out loud.

Hammerhead Sharks
- Named for their hammer-like heads (with two extensions called "cephalofoils").
- Eyes on the edges of each side of the hammer—means there is a huge blind spot directly in front of their nose!

- Found in many oceans around the world.
- Four species found in Sri Lanka: wing-head shark, scalloped hammerhead, great hammerhead, and smooth hammerhead.

Winghead Shark

- Also known as the slender hammerhead.
- Named after hammer-shaped head that can be almost as wide as half its body length.
- Thought to live up to at least twenty years old.

Scalloped Hammerhead

- Found solitary, in pairs, or in huge groups (schools).
- Scalloped hammerhead sharks are caught for their fins and meat.
- Listed as Critically Endangered.

Great Hammerhead

- Largest species of hammerhead shark—maximum length of 20 feet (6.1 meters) and weight of 991 pounds (450 kilograms).
- Nearly straight hammer-shaped head with indent in the middle.
- May live up to forty-four years old.

Smooth Hammerhead Shark

- Found worldwide in coastal, temperate, and tropical waters.
- May live up to twenty years or longer.
- Known to cannibalistically eat smaller members of their own species.

"Ew, they eat one another?!" Dilip said, sticking out his tongue. I laughed, but it was cut short when we heard a bunch of commotion inside the fish market building. It sounded like yelling . . .

CHAPTER NINE

Curious as to why there was so much yelling, we went inside and saw a group of men in matching uniforms shouting with men in bloodied shirts and shorts. I couldn't believe what I was seeing at their feet!

"Adrianna . . . Zev . . . is *that* a shark?" Manisha asked, her face looking a little green at the animal that seemed to be looking at us with its large eyes.

"Yeah . . . but I don't know what kind of shark," Zev answered.

"Adrianna, is this shark in your field notebook?" Punya asked.

I shook my head, my eyes never leaving the animal.

"No. But I'd know this one anywhere," I whispered.

There was no mistaking the giant thresher shark on the floor, nor the pile of what looked to be frozen shark fins in the containers behind it. Thresher sharks are found in all temperate and tropical oceans of the world. It was on my bucket list to see them hunting in action. While most sharks are dangerous at just one end (their mouth), threshers have weaponized their tails to stun fish. The paralyzed animals are then an easy target for these sharks to gobble up. I had only seen videos of them in action, and I'd always hoped for the chance to see one for real. But not like this . . .

The family has three species, but I couldn't tell which one was the one on the floor. The long top half of its tail sagged sadly toward its small mouth, and it was then that I noticed the striking difference between the top and bottom half of the shark—from a slate gray color to a creamy underside—which caught me by surprise. I thought the colors were only this bright underwater!

"Adrianna, we should really get going," Zev said, tugging at my elbow and pulling me out of my trance.

"Zev, what are they saying?" I asked him, ignoring his pleas.

"Those two fishers are being arrested for bringing in that shark. The people in the uniforms are officials of the Department of Fisheries and the Sri Lanka Coast Guard," Zev explained.

"Why are they here?" I continued, probing.

"It's a raid. Sometimes that happens in the fishing markets," Zev said.

"Why are they being arrested? There are other

sharks here, too." I motioned to the other mats. Some people had quickly picked up the corners of their mats and left, clearly unsettled by the raid, the officers present, or both.

Zev listened as the officers and the fishers argued. As he concentrated on that, I took a quick picture of what was unfolding before us. He then turned to me and said, "It's a banned species for capture in Sri Lanka. And they apparently brought almost forty pounds of shark fins with them."

"Illegal ones?" I asked.

"Aren't all shark fins obtained illegally?" Dilip asked.

I shook my head. "Not exactly. Shark finning has a particular definition: the removal of a shark's fins while it is still on the fishing vessel and dumping the rest of the shark overboard. Sometimes fishers bring the shark on land with their fins attached and then take off their fins—but that isn't 'shark finning,' according to the experts' definition. And those fins would be legal."

"Oh, like shark fins for that soup?" Punya asked.

I nodded. "Do you guys have shark fin soup here?"

My friends shrugged their shoulders, Punya mumbling something like "sura puttu." I was about to ask what that meant when fresh yelling made us turn our attention back to the officials, who were now putting handcuffs on the fishers.

"Holy crap!" Zev said. We all looked at him for an explanation. And boy, did we get one. It turned out that the thresher shark the fishers had caught weighed more than five hundred pounds!

"I wonder . . ." I muttered under my breath.

"What, Adrianna?" my friends asked.

"Well, did they accidentally catch this shark and bring it back to the market to sell, or did they go looking for it?" I asked.

"I doubt they targeted this one specific shark, Adrianna. The ocean is very big and sharks, even the biggest ones, like these, are small," Manisha said with a playful roll of her eyes.

I stuck my tongue out. "Not like that! I mean, did they have a specific buyer?"

"Who would want a big shark and some fins?" asked Dilip.

"People who know how much money something like that could make . . ." I said, mostly to myself.

The noise around me started to drown out as I looked around the market to see if I could find the possible buyers if they hadn't already been scared off by the officials. They probably would stand out from the locals and look sort of like tourists . . . sort of like me.

As my eyes scanned the bit of the market I could see, I looked for people who were trying to blend in as much as they could. It wasn't long before I spotted someone who sorely stood out, even though she tried to cover her pale arms with colorful fabric. She had long, light blonde hair in a braid behind her back. I felt a pit grow in my stomach as I realized I knew her.

"Adrianna, what's the matter? You look worried. Are you feeling okay?" Zev asked, once again tugging at my elbow. I pointed at the blonde and said to the group, "I know her! At least, if she is who I think she is, then we have the possible buyers. Poachers. But I need you guys to see if you can spot a tall, tanned guy with tattoos. He might have a hat! And sunglasses!"

"You mean like him?" Manisha asked, pointing to Mr. Muscle Lucky Charms himself. He even had a black hat on, just like the last time. I wondered if it had the fishing lure symbol stitched in gray on the front. I gulped, nervous. I could never forget his face.

When the blonde woman and he met up and chatted, it reminded me of the first time Feye and I had seen them in the hidden mangrove channel back in Cuba.

"Who are they?" Dilip asked, sounding a bit scared. I felt just like he sounded.

"Poachers. And dangerous ones," I said, looking as the woman gave him a hug. She almost seemed friendly when she briefly smiled at him, but the stone-faced mask quickly went back on when the fishers started yelling again as they began to be hauled away.

"They're clever and are okay with hurting people to get the animal they're after," I continued, echoing what Dad's friend Soriano had said back in Cuba.

"Then we should go. Now," Zev insisted.

"One second," I said as I brought the camera up to my face and focused the lens on them. With a snap of the camera, I took a picture of the poachers to show my parents and the camera crew. If the poach-ers were here, it could only mean trouble—maybe they had heard about the Pondicherry shark, too!

I was prepared for the whirring noise of the camera, but I wasn't prepared for the flash that went off. Every face turned to look at our group, including the poachers, whose faces morphed from confused to recognition in a millisecond.

As they came closer to us, it made me wish we had told our parents, the crew, Mr. Savage . . . someone . . . where we were.

CHAPTER TEN

The woman started toward us. I had almost forgotten how tall and muscular she was.

"It's that kid, Sarge!" I heard her yell, with an accent I couldn't place. Had I noticed it the last time our paths crossed?

"Adrianna! Let's go!" Zev whispered, snapping me out of my trance. I looped my camera strap around my neck and took his hand as our group dashed through the people who had gathered to see the result of the raid.

"Split up! Meet back at the hotel!" I said to Manisha, Punya, and Dilip. They nodded and took a left turn at the next aisle while Zev and I took a right—only to hit a dead end.

"We're trapped!" I squeaked. Somehow, we had come across the only closed-off part of this whole marketplace. I looked back and expected to see the blonde woman right behind us. But instead of a poacher, I saw my brother!

"Feye! What are you doing here?"

"I'll explain later. Come on, follow me!"

Once more we ran through the maze of people, eventually finding an open door and bursting onto the beach.

"Don't stop running!" Feye said, looking down at his phone's map.

We ran for a few more minutes until we were all panting and covered in sweat thanks to the humidity.

"Can we at least slow down to a jog now?" I asked.

"I don't think anyone followed us," Zev said.

Feye suddenly stopped with a big sigh, turning to us with furrowed eyebrows.

"What in the world were you thinking, running off like that? Without even telling me!" Feye said. By the twinge of hurt in his voice, I realized my brother was really upset. I didn't realize he cared so much about being included in what I did.

"I'm responsible for you, Adrianna!" he continued, and I frowned. Oh, so he was just worried about getting in trouble with our parents? Typical big brother move.

"She was with me and I know where I'm going," Zev interjected.

"No offense, Zev, but you two are kids," Feye said, exasperation in his voice. "You could've gotten into real trouble and no one would've known where to even begin looking for you!"

"So how did *you* know where to look, *hermano*?" I asked.

He held up his phone. "The find-my-phone app," he said. "And I saw you leave while I was swimming, so I got out of the pool and followed you."

I sighed. "Well . . . thanks, I guess. Things did get a bit out of hand. I didn't realize we would be walking into a raid! I just wanted to take some photos of the sharks for the shark festival."

"The one that hasn't been approved yet?" Feye asked. I knew he didn't mean it in a bad way. He had a point. We hadn't heard back from the network on whether they liked the idea yet.

"The very one," I answered.

"Well, for what it's worth, I like the idea of the shark festival. But why the photos?" Feye asked, continuing to lead us closer to the hotel. I could see the bright pink roof from where we were and I let out a sigh of relief. As I explained to Feye why I wanted to take the photos, I saw his expression change and knew he was impressed. I held up my camera as I told him we also had a photo of the poachers to show our parents and Mr. Savage to alert them of the danger the Pondicherry shark could be in.

"You think they're after it?" Feye questioned.

"Maybe. I don't really know. But surely we weren't the only ones who heard about this super-rare shark that might be in this area," I said.

"Hm . . . well, let me see these pictures. You've given me an idea," he said, motioning for the camera. I unlooped it from around my neck and passed the hunk of bulky technology to him. As he clicked through the photos, his eyebrows danced in what I thought was a mixture of approval and . . . well, something else I couldn't quite place.

"Hey, some of these are really good! But that poacher picture won't be of any use." He passed me back the camera and pointed out the last photo I had taken. Of course it had my finger in the way, so you couldn't see any faces and instead you just saw two pairs of legs and feet.

Oh no!

"But the good photos? If you want, I can share them on my social media feeds and tell people more about shark fishing and trade," Feye said. "Every little bit helps."

We made it to the front doors of our hotel, where Manisha, Dilip, and Punya were already waiting for us.

"We're so glad you're safe!" Manisha yelled, giving us both a big hug. After our hug, I stepped back and stood next to my brother, introducing them to my new friends.

"Feye was just saying our photos might be good enough to post on social media," I explained, making sure everyone was caught up in the conversation.

"There's a huge demand for shark fins in many Asian countries. Maybe sharing another viewpoint could make people think twice about their choices," Feye explained.

"That's a great idea!" I exclaimed, hugging my brother. He was so cool. Sometimes.

"Why are you so passionate about sharks, Adrianna?" Manisha asked.

"Well, because . . . they are so misunderstood. They're not the cutest things to look at, so many people think of them as these monsters. But they're an important part of the ocean's food web and are usually a good indicator of whether or not a habitat is healthy," I explained. "Like, a healthy coral reef usually has many sharks patrolling it!"

"I never thought about it like that," said Punya. Suddenly, her phone started to ring and she glanced at the screen.

"We better go. It's getting late for us. See you tomorrow? We can give you our photos then!" Dilip said.

"I'm gonna head home, too. I've had enough

adventure for one day!" Zev agreed. Feye and I nodded, waving goodbye to the group as they scurried
away from our hotel's door. Once they were out of
sight, Feye turned to me.

"Well, there's only one thing to do now," he said.

"What's that?" I asked, following him into the
lobby and up to the hotel's elevator.

"Try to sneak back into our room without having
to explain to our parents where we've been . . ."

CHAPTER ELEVEN

As soon as we stepped out of the elevator, we saw our dad standing at the door of our hotel room, arms crossed.

Mom rubbed her temples with her slender fingers. "Adrianna, I don't know which is worse: the pain in my arm or the headache you give me whenever you pull stunts like this," she mumbled.

I shot an appreciative glance toward Feye, grateful he hadn't told our parents about the run-in with the poachers we'd seen in Cuba. With no photographic proof to back up my claim, there was no point. Plus, if they had believed me, they wouldn't let me out of their sight for a second the rest of our time here. I couldn't have that.

Instead, Feye had just told them I had run off to the market to take pictures of the sharks there for the possible shark festival. He even left Zev out of it! I was very thankful in that moment to a brother who often had my back and supported my plans—however foolish they might be.

"I'm sorry, Mom," I whispered. "It was a reckless thing for me to do."

"And irresponsible! I thought you had grown up a little during our Cuba trip," Dad said.

I hung my head down and that's when Feye put a strong, reassuring hand on my shoulder.

"Sure, she messed up," he said. "But she has an amazing idea."

"And Feye has a good idea about sharing the photos on his social media channels!" I chimed in.

"Feye, we have to be careful about these posts.

We can't blame the fishers for this," Dad said.

"We don't want to offend anyone," my mom continued. "Fishermen make everyday decisions about where to fish and what to catch. The decline of sharks is a problem that affects fisheries, and people's livelihoods. We need to work together with them to support sustainable fishing practices— something that benefits them and helps conserve our oceans in the long run."

"So, what do you think we should do?" Feye asked Mom.

After a bit of discussion, it was Dad who came up with a great idea to work with my shark photography plan. We'd do a series of portrait photographs of the fishermen. Alongside the portraits would be a little bit about why they are proud to be fishers and their relationship with the ocean.

"This might actually work!" Feye smiled.

"I'll call Mr. Savage. Although he and the crew

might be downstairs eating dinner, given the time," Dad said. He picked up the phone and dialed, listened for a while, then frowned. "It's just ringing. He must not be in his room," Dad said.

"Well, guess we just have to go downstairs and find him!" I declared, motioning toward the door with big hand gestures. *Come on,* familia *Villalobos! Hustle!*

After what felt like forever, I was able to wrangle my dad and brother out of our hotel room and into the elevator that would take us to the ground floor, where the restaurant was. If I thought it would be hard to spot our crew, I was wrong. I could easily make out Connor's loud Australian accent as he argued with Mark and Alice that he could have two servings of everything if he pleased.

"Ah! If it isn't our star family!" Mr. Savage said, standing up and shaking my father's hand. "Pull up a chair and join us."

We sat down and looked at the feast before us. A multitude of dishes in bright greens, yellows, reds, and oranges were piled high on stark white plates, making my mouth water as each crew member took a heaping spoonful of each and added it to their own plate. I grabbed a menu and, as I expected from an island in the Indian Ocean, seafood was the key ingredient in most of the Sri Lankan cuisine before us. I tried to identify some of the food on the table: *fish ambul thiyal, kottu roti, kukul mas curry, lamprais* . . . jeez, how much were these guys eating?!

"Have y'all eaten dinner yet?" Alice asked, stabbing a piece of roti with her fork and quickly taking it away from the communal pile.

"The kids just got back from an adventure to the fish market," Dad said, jerking his head toward us. "Adrianna was especially keen to tell you guys about it."

"Oh! The one down the road a fair way?" Mark asked, some rice coming out of his full mouth. He held up a hand in apology.

"That's the one!" I beamed, getting my camera ready to show them my photography. I might not always get the shot—hello, finger in my most important photo yet—but the ones I did manage to get from the market made me feel super proud.

"We're filming there the day after tomorrow," Mr. Savage said. He turned to me. "You getting into the mindset of a producer and staking out our film sites?" Everyone at the table laughed.

I shook my head. "Not quite. I had another idea, though."

"More ideas?" Connor said.

I told them about my feelings after the outburst I had at the restaurant, the elephant encounter, and how I saw people coexisting with these beautiful creatures, which got me thinking about how culturally important they are in this part of the world. I knew we were still waiting to hear back from the network to see if the Shark Appreciation Festival would even happen, but I hoped the photo gallery idea of sharks and fishermen would add to it. Mark and Alice took my camera and went through my photos. Every now and then they would nod and show the photo to Mr. Savage, who would comment about the lighting or the angle.

"I think it'd be a really cool segment for the show," I finished. "Our family working together with the local community to learn about their culture and educate them about sharks through their own scientists and us."

Feye then took over, showing how many followers he had on his various social media accounts and how having a series of photos using specific hashtags like #wildlife or #sharks would bring attention to what we were doing in Sri Lanka. Dad went on to explain how to further the reach in the local area by working with both the fishermen and the scientists to share their stories.

Mr. Savage was quiet for a long time after we finished telling him our ideas. He had put his fork down halfway through my speech and had stopped chewing to give us his full attention. It felt nice, to be respected enough by an adult to have them listen wholeheartedly. I kind of felt a bit more grown-up myself!

"The network hasn't made a final decision on the shark festival, as you know," said Mr. Savage. Oh no, I could feel a wave of disappointment coming on. "But I think this might just be the thing they need to hear to give us the go-ahead."

My face broke out into a huge grin as I clapped my hands with enthusiasm. He liked the idea!

"I'm going to call the network again to tell them what you've come up with and see where they stand," he continued. "Since we are still waiting to hear on whether this critter in the restaurant is the Pondicherry shark or not, we can explore this avenue until then. Between the elephants, sea snakes, and this? If we can pull this off . . . oh!"

His freckled, pale hand slammed against the table, making everyone's glasses rattle and shake. Some even spilled some liquid over their edges.

"This is going to be a huge hit if we pull it off. I can just see it. 'Family fights for monster's rights.' It's perfect!"

I cringed as Mr. Savage called sharks "monsters" since that was the exact opposite of what I wanted people to think of them as. But if it got us the green light from the network, well, could I really complain?

Mr. Savage picked up his plate, scooped up some more food to top it off, and stood up. "Right. I'm calling it a night, guys. I've got a few phone calls to make."

We turned back to the rest of the crew. "So . . . what do you guys think?" I asked, realizing not one of them had said anything. Maybe it was because they were starving and just too hungry to speak.

Alice was the first to speak. "My thoughts?"

I nodded, encouraging her to go on.

"If you don't want to go down the wildlife conservationist route, you have one keen eye for photography!"

I blushed at the compliment. That was high praise coming from someone as talented as Alice!

"I second her, Adrianna. You really have a gift! We'll have to talk Savage into getting you to hold a GoPro or something more often," Mark agreed, his plate and mouth finally empty.

"Not my area of expertise at all," Connor said. "But I know a good photo when I see one. And I see a couple there."

"You said your friends took some photos as well?" Alice asked.

"Yeah. Each one of us had a camera so we could cover more ground," I explained.

"It was like a secret mission of sorts." Feye smirked.

"Definitely want to see those. We can identify the sharks, and when we go out to get footage, we can prioritize getting live-action shots of those animals for comparison!" Alice nodded to herself.

"Better alive than dead," chimed in Mark.

CHAPTER TWELVE

Mr. Savage wasn't at his usual seat at our table during breakfast the next morning. I had been hoping to learn whether or not our Shark Appreciation Festival was a go.

"Do you think Mr. Savage has an answer yet?" I asked as Mom made up a plate of food for me.

"Maybe. But regardless if it is a yes or no, we are so proud of you, Adrianna," Dad said as he smiled at me. He already had his morning cup of coffee and seemed a lot more alert than Mom, who was sipping away slowly at her tea. She had woken up with no pain from the jellyfish sting and the only evidence that anything had ever happened was a pink mark on her arm.

Mom nodded. "You really showed initiative by taking responsibility for your emotional outburst the other day and harnessing those frustrated emotions into some positive action."

She turned to Dad. "Our little girl is growing up! Right before our eyes!"

I rolled my eyes.

We all ate in silence for a few minutes, the only noise at our table the slurping of drinks or the clatter of silverware against our emptying plates. I slowly drank my milk, happy to have something cold to refresh my dry throat. As I put my glass back down, I took a second to breathe in the spices that hung in the air like a yummy perfume. I looked at the colorful dishes on everyone's table, the conversations a mixture of English, Sinhala, Tamil, and some other languages that sounded like music coming out of their speakers' mouths.

One voice in particular cut through the melody. "Good morning, everyone! How are we doing today?" Mr. Savage boomed, suddenly quieting those around us.

Different from his usual garments, he wore a flashy black outfit that shimmered in the lights. I looked at the clothes the camera crew wore to see if we had to go back upstairs to change. No one told us we had to look fancy today! I was in an old khaki shirt, my swimsuit, and dirty shorts, so if we were going to some party, I at least wanted to look kind of nice.

Before any of us could respond, Mr. Savage began speaking again. "Do we want to hear some amazing news? Or today's itinerary?"

"The amazing news, of course!" I shouted. I quickly clapped my hands over my mouth. That had been a little louder than I intended.

"You heard my sister! The news!" Feye parroted,

play-punching my arm to let me know it was okay I had been too loud.

"The network loved the ideas! So today I'll be heading into town and working with some local vendors to find where we can set up this amazing festival," Mr. Savage said, and then turned to me and winked. "Including your photo gallery idea."

I instantly brightened up and ripped my hands away from my face. Hooray! Yes! This was just the news I needed to hear to continue to prove myself as a part of the *Wild Survival!* team.

Mr. Savage turned to Alice, Mark, and Connor. "Evelyn told me about how Adrianna and Manil's kid Zev came across some Sri Lankan elephants. Manil knows where that particular water hole is, so I want him to lead the adults back there for some photos and captivating footage of them among these animals."

Wait, the adults? Are Feye and I included in that?

"What about us, Mr. Savage?" asked Feye, who must've been reading my thoughts.

"Those photos your sister took in the market the other day gave me an idea." Mr. Savage winked. As if by magic, his hand dipped into a bag that he held by his side that I hadn't seen before. In went a bare hand, out came a hand with two GoPros. "I had a chat with Alice and Mark and we all agree that getting some footage shot by you and Adrianna would be good for bits of the show, promos, and social media," he said as he handed us each a camera. "We'll call it 'Villalobos Vision'!"

I giggled at the name.

But Feye wasn't convinced. "So, let me get this straight. No elephants for A and me?"

Mr. Savage shook his head, his face going a bit red at being further questioned. "Not today. Heard there are some aggressive bulls around and your parents made the decision to keep you two away from the elephants. Perfect for filming . . . but also for accidently squishing kids. So that's a no for you guys." His tone changed, as if he was displeased with what our parents said.

After what had happened to me in Cuba, I knew they were being a bit stricter with what animals we were interacting with. I had heard them raising their voices while talking about this with Mr. Savage, who said it could ruin the show if they chose to leave us out of pivotal moments.

"Where do we go, then?" I asked, desperate to change the sore subject.

"How about snorkeling at a beach?" Mom piped up.

"Like the one near the fish market?" Feye offered.

"Might get some good shots of animals eating tossed-over scraps," Dad said, nodding.

"Dr. Chandrika is out there today. You guys can meet up with her. Stay out of trouble," Mom warned.

"Yes, Mom," we answered in unison.

We finished our breakfast quickly and kissed our parents goodbye. With the GoPros still in hand, we raced upstairs to grab some towels and our wet suits before heading outside toward the fish market.

"Think we'll see anything cool?" I asked Feye, who was busy taking a video for his "thousands of worldwide fans." He finished with a wink to the camera and then turned to me and shrugged.

"Who knows. With you around, probably. Interesting stuff always finds you," my big brother teased.

The walk to the market felt shorter than yesterday's walk, maybe because we went the direct way instead of through dirt backroads to avoid possibly being seen by the poachers. As we got closer, I could make out the distinctive smell of not-quite-dried fish on the yellowy sand of the beach. The sun wasn't as intense as yesterday's, but I was glad for the coverage our wet suits would give us. And after my mom's run-in with a jellyfish, we wanted to make sure we were as protected as possible.

Now at the beach, we chose to walk away from the fish market smell. Farther down the beach we could see people lying out on towels and tanning, fruity drinks in their hands.

"Adrianna?" I heard a male voice say as we got closer to the water's edge. I looked around and spotted Dilip, who was waving hello and coming toward us.

"Feye, you remember Dilip, right?" I said.

"Yeah, I remember. Hey, Dilip," Feye said curtly, glancing at the water eagerly.

"What are you doing here?" I asked, ignoring my brother's pleading look to hurry this conversation up.

"My father is a fisher. He's dropping off his catch inside," he answered, pointing toward the building we all had run away from yesterday. "What about you?"

I held up the GoPro. "Filming, for the show. We were just going for a quick snorkel. Have you swum here before?"

Dilip nodded. "Sure, plenty of times. There are some cool things to see around the coral here."

"Like?" I asked.

"Sea snakes, for one."

I saw Feye's skin instantly prickle up. He was fine with land snakes . . . but sea snakes scared him. I tried to get him to explain it to me once, but he just shut me down by putting his headphones on. Typical older brother move.

"That would be awesome to see, right, Feye?" I asked, trying to calm him down by reaching out for his hand. He hesitated for a second before taking it, as if wondering if his "coolness" would go down a smidge in front of Dilip for holding my hand.

"Dad's going to be busy for a while. Mind if I join you?" Dilip asked.

I looked at Feye, who shrugged.

"Sure. Just try to stay out of the way of the GoPro," Feye said. With that, my brother and I changed into our wet suits and we all went into the water.

"We only have to swim a little bit before getting to the coral heads around here," Dilip explained, spitting water out of his mouth and taking a deep breath before diving under the waves, motioning for us to follow him. Without another word, Feye and I made sure to turn our "Villalobos Vision" on, and each took one side of Dilip so we wouldn't accidental capture him on our film.

As I swam forward and looked down, all I saw at first was the sandy bottom with funky patterns dancing on it from the sun above us. After a few more kicks, rocks started to litter my view. The rocks turned into bigger boulders and then coral patches. Fish of every color darted between the structures, hiding from us as we came closer. Big fish, small fish, it was a kaleidoscope of mesmerizing hues.

"Ah, here's one!" we heard Dilip yell out from the surface, and we turned to see him pointing to an animal that . . . well, looked like a snake; there was no denying that! As it swam in an S-shaped pattern, I could see the black-and-white banding coming our way.

"Is that a sea snake or a snake that jumped from a nearby tree and just happens to know how to swim?" Feye asked, his head above the water's surface.

"It's a banded sea krait! These are pretty common around here," Dilip said.

BANDED SEA KRAIT

- These snakes have black stripes along their body and a yellow snout.

- They spend most of their time in the water but can also be found on land.

- Eels and small fish are the sea krait's main prey.

- Sea kraits have a paddle-like tail that helps them swim through the water.

I didn't bring my head out of the water until the snake had safely passed, its small eyes checking me out but otherwise leaving me alone as it minded its own business.

"Are they poisonous?" Feye asked.

I shook my head. "Poisonous, no," I said. "Venomous, yes."

"What's the difference?" asked Dilip.

"Poison gets into the body by you swallowing or inhaling it. Or even absorbing it through your skin. Venom is injected into the body, like through a bite or sting," I said.

"Are there animals that are both?" Dilip asked, intrigued.

"Sometimes. At the zoo in our aquarium portion, we have an exhibit for the blue-ringed octopus, which is both poisonous and venomous," I said. "Venomous when it bites things with its beak, but also poisonous if you swallow it."

Dilip looked at me in awe, and then to Feye, who rolled his eyes. "My sister, the walking encyclopedia."

Before I could say something snarky in return, I took a deep breath and went back to snorkeling. We could talk on land! I wanted to take every opportunity I could to see what was in Sri Lankan waters.

But as I swam ahead of Dilip and my brother, I was horrified at what I saw. Popping my head up and out of the water, I yelled out to the guys, who swam quickly to me. I pointed down below us and looked at Dilip.

"How long have these been here?" I asked, and both Feye and Dilip submerged their heads to see the piles of floating fishing ropes and lines beneath our feet, nearly invisible in the dim light. Entangled in them were fish, or what remained of fish, and other animals I couldn't quite make out.

"Ghost fishing. I've only read about it, but have never seen it," Feye said with a sad tone in his voice.

"What's ghost fishing?" Dilip asked.

"It's when there is discarded, lost, or abandoned fishing gear in the marine environment that still is catching animals," Feye explained. "It's something that happens all over the world, not just here."

I dipped my head under again, not believing how much discarded gear there was. I, too, had only read about ghost fishing and never seen it in person. Every year millions of marine animals get caught in this kind of waste, like fish, sharks, whales, seals, turtles, and even birds. I knew we could report abandoned fishing gear back at home, but what about here?

A sudden movement in the net caught my eye, and with another deep breath, like I saw Zev take before he went free diving, I dove underwater and kicked to get closer to the pile of stuff. There, tangled in the clear lines, was a green sea turtle, desperately wiggling back and forth to get free. I usually only saw them wriggle around so much when they were clambering onto land to sunbathe.

The stinging in my chest reminded me that I wasn't a fish and needed to take a breath. Kicking back up to the surface, I looked at the guys as I gasped and filled my lungs with air.

"There's a turtle stuck in the line!" I said. "We have to get it out!"

"It could bite you!" Feye said.

"When have you heard of a sea turtle biting someone?" I argued.

Feye looked stumped.

"Mom and Dad always say to 'do the right thing.' We can't just leave it down there to drown," I said. Sea turtles aren't like fish. They need to come up to the surface to breathe. I knew my brother wouldn't disagree with me on that. He loved animals as much as I did.

"We don't even have anything to cut it loose with, A," Feye said, sighing.

"I do!" Dilip said, rummaging in his pocket and producing a sharp knife.

Feye and I did a double take.

"What?" asked Dilip. "It's a dive knife. I have it when I go fishing with my dad in case the line gets caught on stuff and we have to cut it off."

"That's perfect!" I said, thankful that we had run into Dilip.

"Well, nice knowing you, Dilip!" Feye said, motioning toward the pile where the sea turtle was wriggling.

"I'm not going down there! I can't hold my breath that long," Dilip said.

I grabbed the knife from him and clipped the GoPro to my shoulder so the camera could see everything. My very own animal rescue! "I'll do it," I said.

Before Feye or Dilip could stop me, I took another deep breath and swam down to the poor sea turtle, which by now had slowed its wriggling a bit. *It must be running out of oxygen. I gotta hurry!*

It was harder to cut through the lines with the knife than I had expected, and after only cutting through two of the four holding the sea turtle down, my lungs demanded I go back up for air. With a few powerful kicks I broke through to the surface and gulped in a few bits of air. I tuned out Feye and Dilip's concerned questions. The turtle was running out of time. I took a final big gulp of air and headed back under the water.

When I was with the sea turtle again, I tried my hardest to go as fast as I could in cutting the lines before I ran out of air again. I felt the line *snap!* as it got cut into two bits. I figured I could just tug the turtle out of the few remaining lines so as not to waste more time. My chest burned, but I didn't want to quit now. The turtle had stopped moving. I reached for the turtle and gently pulled it out from the cut lines.

One second the turtle was lying limp in the ocean's current and the next it was thrashing in my hand trying to free itself from my grip. The motion allowed the turtle to wiggle backward out of my grasp and the remaining lines around it. Without a second glance behind it, the small reptile shot out of my hand and into the open ocean.

The shock of the turtle suddenly coming back to life caused me to let out a "Wow!" I took in a big mouthful of salty water by accident. My chest burned and I realized I was in trouble. I kicked my legs, which felt strangely heavy now, and tried to focus on the bright sunlight of the surface above.

Am I going to drown?

CHAPTER THIRTEEN

A few bubbles escaped my mouth and they gently floated up to the surface, where sunbeams scattered every which way now that the sun was out in full force. I could even feel its warmth from down here, and it was making me a bit sleepy.

I willed my legs to kick upward, despite feeling tired, and made my arms sort of do a swimming motion, even though it felt like I was trying to move through Jell-O.

I thought I could hear yelling from above the waves, but I couldn't be sure. There was movement above me, and suddenly I realized Feye was diving down toward me. With what little energy I had left, I reached for my brother's hand with my fingertips— as far as they could go—and could have cried from joy when his hand grabbed mine and rapidly pulled me up.

My head felt stuffy as we broke through the Jell-O and I hit the fresh air. My stomach churned and I heaved up some of the ocean water I had swallowed.

"Adrianna!" Feye said, swimming us toward the shore. "Are you okay?"

I squinted up at my brother, the sun making it hard to see much of him aside from a fuzzy outline.

"I'm okay," I whispered, my throat feeling dry as a desert.

"What happened?! I saw you struggling to come up," Feye said.

"I freed the sea turtle, Feye. But then I accidentally swallowed a lot of water," I explained.

"Help, someone help!" Dilip yelled as we reached the sand. He helped Feye pull me onto the sand.

A few of the adults looked up from their mats and towels and I suddenly recognized one of the adults who had come up to us in a hurry. It was Dr. Chandrika, wearing a bright pink one-piece swimsuit. "What happened?" she asked.

"She saw a sea turtle stuck in some fishing lines so she cut it loose, but she stayed down too long and swallowed a lot of water," Dilip explained.

Another woman on the beach fished a phone out of her backpack. Was she calling for the doctors?

"Hi, sweetheart," Dr. Chandrika said to me, her eyes now focused on me. My vision was still blurry, even though I was no longer looking directly into the sun. Was I going blind?

"Remember me? The woman over there is my partner, Helen. I'm going to see if we can try to help you, okay?" she said.

I nodded silently.

She turned to my brother. "Where are your parents? Are they here on the beach?"

I couldn't make out what Feye said. My body started to feel achy, as if I had run for a really long time.

"Can you tell me about the sea turtle?" Dr. Chandrika asked loudly. Maybe I hadn't heard her the first time.

Focus, Adrianna. What kind of sea turtle was it?

"I'm pretty sure it was a green sea turtle," I managed to croak out.

"How do you know?" Dilip asked.

It took every bit of energy I had to shrug. "They're my favorite," I said. My tongue felt fuzzy, like it was taking up my whole mouth. And dry . . . so dry.

"Did you just inhale a lot of water when coming back up after rescuing the turtle?" Dr. Chandrika asked.

I nodded again, realizing I had no control of my eyelids, as they were dropping closed no matter how much I willed them to stay open.

"Do you think you spat it back up?" Dr. Chandrika said. She sounded so far away.

"I think she did!" Feye answered.

I could feel a slight breeze brushing past my hot cheeks. "You're going to be just fine" was the last thing I heard before blackness tugged me under.

I had no idea how I got into my hotel bed or when my parents had arrived at my bedside. Dr. Chandrika, Ms. Helen, and Feye all brought me to the hotel, where my parents laid me down in bed to rest. Our medic, Miguel, checked me over to make sure I had no water in my lungs. Thankfully I didn't, but I had one heck of a sore throat and dry mouth.

"Just drink a ton of water and maybe stay

away from super-spicy foods for a while." Miguel winked while patting my leg and leaving our hotel room.

"What you did was kind of cool, even if you almost died," Feye let slip out before slamming a hand over his mouth. My parents looked at him, eyebrows raised. "Not what I meant! I meant her rescuing the turtle was cool, not the almost drowning bit."

"We know what you meant," Dad said.

"Thanks for helping me." I looked at my brother, feeling a bit better already.

"Since you're out of the woods and okay, I guess we can hear all about it now, *mi tesoro*," Dad said, reaching over and squeezing my hand. I squeezed it back. Feye had filled my parents in on what had happened while I rested, and while they were mad that I hadn't been more careful, they weren't disappointed at the fact I was trying to do the right thing by helping an animal out.

Feye hesitatingly nodded to me as I told them my side of the story. By the end, they were impressed that we were able to get the sea turtle out alive.

"Hey, Dad? I have a question," I asked, wanting to clear something up.

"What's that, Adrianna?" he asked.

"Can a sea turtle bite you?"

"Yes, they can! Sea turtles have really strong jaws and very sharp beaks. I've never been bitten, but I've heard their bite can be quite painful and can lead to bruises or even broken bones in some extreme cases."

Feye smirked, clearly pleased he had been right. I shrugged. "Well, I didn't get bitten, at least!" I said.

My dad kissed me on my forehead. "Get some rest. We're going back to visit the restaurant with the possible Pondicherry shark for dinner tonight. If you're feeling up to it, you can come with us. Dr. Chandrika is going to bring the results of the DNA test to share."

I pulled off my sheets. "Oh, I'll be up to it!" I said. There was no way that I'd miss that!

CHAPTER FOURTEEN

After an afternoon nap, I felt much better. I couldn't wait to see what Dr. Chandrika had to say. When we got to the restaurant, Mrs. Gamage, one of the restaurant owners, invited us inside.

"Come, come, sit," she said, just like last time. She pointed to the fridge near the door to see if anyone wanted a drink. We shook out heads and she led us to a table close to the shark. Could this shark really be the rare Pondicherry?

I couldn't help but notice that the bright green skirt and shirt outfit Mrs. Gamage had on matched the headscarf on her head that kept her thick black hair off her shoulders. With Mr. Manil there as our interpreter, I asked him to tell her I liked her red lipstick—something I wished I had been able to tell her the first time we had met. He smiled and relayed my comment to her, which in turn made her smile and bow her head in thanks.

Mr. Gamage soon came out from the back with some glasses and bottled water, pouring us each a tall glass.

My eyes slid over to the tank next to us. There were still no colorful rocks, coral, plants, or other fish in the aquarium. The gray shark swam to one end and then turned around and came back. Again and again and again. I could feel my heart breaking. But just then the door opened and Dr. Chandrika came in with a stack of papers—the DNA results!

"Thank you again, Mr. and Mrs. Gamage, for allowing us to all have a conversation about this rare shark you have in your possession," said Mr. Savage. He had come along to help persuade the Gamages to allow us to release the shark into the wild. I didn't know if that meant he was going to come up with a really good argument as to why they should let us have it or if he was going to pay them.

"*Possible* rare shark," Dad corrected.

Dr. Chandrika shook her head as she sat down and pushed the paper toward my family. "No, he's correct. The DNA match came in—it's a Pondicherry shark."

Feye and I gasped. My mom, dad, and Mr. Savage pored over the results. After a few silent minutes of passing all the documents around, they looked up at Mr. Gamage.

"We just wanted to stress the importance of what this shark represents for not only Sri Lanka, but our oceans," Mr. Savage started. He took out a piece of paper my family had prepared earlier today listing all the reasons why sharks mattered. "'As top predators, sharks help manage our healthy ocean ecosystems by feeding on the animals lower down in the food web.'"

"And other big animals, like dolphins or tuna, they can't do that?" Mr. Manil translated Mr. Gamage's words for us.

"Not quite in the same way that sharks do," Dad said, stepping in as Mr. Savage looked at him for guidance. He only really knew what was written on the page we had given him.

"What my husband is trying to say is that predators like sharks not only affect how many animals there are of a single species, but they control where they go in a habitat through intimidation," Mom chimed in.

"So the sharks bully other fish?" Mrs. Gamage asked, and Mr. Manil translated for us.

"Not quite," Mom said. "Fear of being eaten causes some animals to alter where they go and how often they go there. This influences the overall community's structure for that habitat and it increases the animal diversity of the ecosystem."

"Dolphins aren't as scary." Mr. Gamage nodded.

"And dolphins aren't as messy eaters, either," I said. This shark enthusiast wasn't going to sit back and be quiet during this conversation! The Gamages looked to me and I looked at my parents for their approval to continue. After a quick nod from my mom, I went on to explain how predators like sharks help provide food for scavengers, since they always leave scraps when they eat.

We continued talking about how balanced ecosystems had healthy shark numbers, and exchanging stories about shark fishing in the community, shark finning, and how rare shark bites are in Sri Lanka.

"The numbers might show that shark attacks are rare worldwide or here in Sri Lanka, but it means nothing when you are one of those numbers," Mr. Gamage said. His expression grew solemn. He stood up and walked toward a wall filled with photos. He pulled a framed picture off the wall and returned to sit with us. The edges of the photograph inside were frayed and yellowed, and it showed two men with their arms around each other, smiling into the camera.

"This is my brother. He was bitten by a shark seven years ago while swimming," Mr. Gamage said through Mr. Manil. He pointed to the man on the left with a black shirt and white shorts. He and Mr. Gamage looked like twins, both wearing their hair short and shaggy toward the middle. I could just make out an earring on the brother's left ear.

"It wouldn't let him go. It dragged him

underwater, bit a big chunk out of his leg. If you ask me, one less shark in the ocean is a good thing," Mr. Gamage said. He nodded curtly.

There was a heavy silence in our group as Mr. Manil finished translating. Everyone took sips of water out of their glass as they tried to figure out what to say next. None of us had been bitten by a shark . . . but I knew a similar fear.

"I'm so sorry about your brother, Mr. Gamage," I said. "None of us know what it's like to get bitten by a shark, or to lose a loved one like that. But I was recently bitten and dragged by a large crocodile, so I know the fear of not knowing what is going on, of wondering if you're going to live and see your family again." I paused to let Mr. Manil finish translating for me.

I stood up and moved my long dress to the side so the Gamages could see my fading bite scars. The little bit of color I had gotten in Sri Lanka had made the scarring not so stark against the rest of my skin. "It bit me in a freak accident while we were scuba diving and filming for our last show. At one point, I didn't know if I would have a leg left."

There was a pause as Mr. Manil interpreted. Mrs. Gamage gasped, her hand trying to muffle the sound as it came out her mouth. Mr. Gamage leaned closer to see my leg.

"Did it hurt a lot?" he asked softly.

I nodded.

"Do you have nightmares?" he asked.

"I've had one or two. But now all of it feels like it was just a bad dream. The scars remind me, though," I answered.

"I'm sorry," Mrs. Gamage said. I looked up to see her eyes shiny, brimming with tears.

"It's okay. It's nobody's fault," I said.

"It's the crocodile's fault," Mr. Gamage said, straightening up and sitting upright in his seat.

"Nope. Not even the crocodile's fault," I said, standing firm and allowing my skirt to drop and re-hide my bare legs. "It was just doing what predators do. The same as sharks."

Before Mr. Gamage could say anything else, I continued, "I know it hurts and it's scary. But we really need an ocean full of sharks to have a healthy ocean. And we need a healthy ocean not just for our health, but for our pocketbooks. Without sharks, you won't have fresh, delicious fish on your menu."

The Gamages seemed to ponder this as Mr. Manil translated for me.

"As your daughter says, fishing for sharks brings food to the table and money into our pockets. Why would we stop that?" Mr. Gamage asked.

"There are other ways to make money from

sharks!" Feye said, also not wanting to be left out of the conversation.

"Such as?" Mrs. Gamage asked.

"Ecotourism. People pay a lot of money to snorkel and dive with sharks," Dr. Chandrika said. "It's a billion-dollar industry worldwide. Not only do they pay money to swim with the sharks, they have to spend money in the local area, too, for food and a place to stay."

Mr. Gamage shook his head. "No one would swim with sharks here. I certainly have no interest being in the water with those monsters."

"This is a lot of talk. What if we show you what we mean, instead?" Mr. Savage interrupted. Everyone turned to look at him.

"The Villalobos family and Dr. Chandrika are proposing a Shark Appreciation Festival in the community. Adrianna has a keen eye for photography and she's hosting a gallery showing live versus dead sharks and how . . ." He trailed off, looking at me to better explain the gallery idea.

"To showcase how sharks' beauty is better appreciated while they are alive and in their environment rather than dead," I said.

"Right. That," Mr. Savage said with a snap of his fingers. "We have a venue, we have the ability to film it, and we're gathering public interest from local scientists to come and give talks. Dr. Chandrika has been asking fishermen if they're willing to have their photos taken to share their story on how their lives are intertwined with the ocean . . . they've pretty much all said yes! I say we add to that and have a community-wide snorkeling trip for locals to swim with the sharks, led by the Villalobos family. Dr. Chandrika, what do you think?"

She nodded. "I think swimming with sharks is a great idea. There are some harmless ones here, like the bamboo sharks, cat sharks, the leopard shark, and whale sharks. And I have some sharks that need releasing from the Waves of Action research trials since we are done with their experiments, so it will be a whole celebration."

Dad looked at me and winked. "I think that's a *brillante idea*."

Mr. Gamage did not look convinced. "Where would you do this?"

"Well, how about the beach right near the fish market?" Dr. Chandrika said. "It's near the Waves of Action headquarters."

A dark look passed over Mr. Gamage, and Mrs. Gamage gasped as Mr. Manil translated.

"That's where his brother was bitten," Mrs. Gamage explained.

There was a long pause before Mr. Savage spoke up. "Think about it as a memorial swim, for your brother," he said.

"Oh, he's not dead," Mrs. Gamage clarified. "He

has a fake leg and is very scared of the water now."

"That is why we will not be going," Mr. Gamage said, still angry.

"It might help," I offered. Everyone stared at me. "I was a little bit afraid of the water after my crocodile bite, too. But it helped to go back in the water with my family." I looked at Feye, who smiled, probably remembering the same memories I was. Of him being right outside the door as I took my first bath, as I dipped my toes into the pool for the first time and dunked my head underwater while holding his hand. He was even there the first time I went swimming at the beach and at a lake on the zoo's property at night. If it wasn't for my brother's support . . . I might still be afraid of the water. And I can't imagine missing out on all the watery fun I will still have in my life.

Mr. Gamage looked at me and nodded, ending the night's conversation, saying he couldn't promise whether or not they would show up.

"And what about concluding the festival with a shark release?" Mr. Savage probed. He nodded toward the Pondicherry in the tank next to us.

"We'll see," Mr. Gamage said.

"Mr. Gamage, how about we do a trade?" Dr. Chandrika proposed. We all turned to look at her.

"We're listening," said Mrs. Gamage.

"Your delicious food isn't the only thing bringing people to your restaurant—this shark attracts diners, too! So, what if we release the shark and I revamp your aquarium? I am happy to donate some beautifully colored fish and other sea creatures we have in my headquarters that are sure to get people talking!"

Mr. Gamage looked thoughtful. He then looked to his wife for a moment before responding. "We have much to discuss. Please give us time to think about it."

We all got up, thanked the Gamages for their time, and left the dimly lit restaurant.

Dad came up from behind me and put a strong hand on my shoulder. "Proud of you, *mi hija*."

CHAPTER FIFTEEN

"*¿Mamá, puedes decirme otra vez?*" Feye asked, showing that he, too, had forgotten who we were going to be talking to during today's TV shoot segment. As he moved, Connor took hold of both his shoulders to keep him from wriggling. Both Feye and I wore our khaki zoo shirts that had SACRED SANCTUARY AND ZOOLOGICAL PARK embroidered in green on a pocket where Connor was trying to clip Feye's microphone.

"Feye, *tienes que escucharme*. We're going to meet up with Dr. Chandrika at the Waves of Action headquarters to talk about the festival," Mom said, rolling her eyes in mock annoyance at Feye not paying attention to her.

"And see the sharks in her aquarium, right, *Mami*?" I asked. Connor was now with me, fastening the small microphone onto my shirt as I looked at my mom for the correct answer. She nodded, busy applying some light makeup on her face.

"There!" Connor declared, standing up from kneeling in front of me. "You're ready." He tugged on some headphones and gave me a thumbs-up to signal for me to test the equipment.

"Testing, one, two, three," I said and saw Connor nod in approval.

"Alright, we're good to go!" Dad said, clapping. "Let's meet up with Dr. Chandrika. I'm excited to hear what she's got to say!"

Not skipping another beat, we headed out to the

elevator and down the road, toward the fishy smell that clung to the early morning air. The battery pack in the back pocket of my pants felt heavy, slapping against me with every step I took.

As we walked past the market, I soaked in the sights. Soon our trip to Sri Lanka would be coming to an end, and I wanted to remember as much as I possibly could.

People zoomed past us on red and gray bikes, some with baskets already full of fish from the market. A slight breeze rustled the bright green leaves of the trees that lined the busy street. For how early it was, I was surprised by how many people were out and about, dressed in bright clothing that matched the flowers blossoming in the trees. Around me I could hear a symphony of people talking, music, and car horns. Behind one of the trees I could see a bright yellow house with a family out on their porch hanging laundry. I spied red shirts, blue shorts, orange towels, and a little boy who saw me watching and waved hello. Smiling, I waved back as we continued down the road.

"Hmm, nothing better than the smell of fish in the morning," Feye said, pretending to gag.

"Feye," Dad warned.

Feye grumbled and fell back from the group. I watched him slow down, unnoticed by our parents as they talked to Mr. Savage. Deciding to not leave him alone, I joined him as we all entered a building near where the fish market was. There we saw Dr. Chandrika, who waved a welcome. Next to her were Alice and Mark, ready with their equipment.

"Hello, Villalobos family!" said Dr. Chandrika, giving us all a huge individual hug. "I am so excited you wanted to learn more about the marine conservation work I'm doing in Sri Lanka."

Alice and Mark followed behind us, cameras softly whirring as they focused on different things—my parents' faces, the corridors of the building as we walked from room to room, the hand movements they were all making. Feye and I stood back quietly as the talk between the adults got increasingly filled with big, technical words neither of us could understand.

"Recently, Sri Lanka teamed up with Senegal to further protect some shark species," said Dr. Chandrika. "We have a few juvenile leopard sharks I'd love to show Adrianna, actually."

Wait a minute! That shark name sounded familiar! Reaching into my other back pocket, I pulled out my field notebook and flipped to where I had written down a few shark names. Sure enough, there was the leopard shark!

Leopard Shark (Stegostoma tigrinum)
- Also known as the zebra shark.

- Known to undergo dramatic change of color from a "zebra" pattern in the juvenile to a "leopard" pattern in the adult stage.

- Feeds on small fish, snails, sea urchins, crabs, etc.

- Confused with *Triakis semifasciata* (see below).

Wait . . . two of them? I read down.

Leopard Shark (Triakis semifasciata)

- Has dark, saddle-shaped splotches on its upper body.

- One of the most common sharks found along the coast of California.

- Is seen in schools.

- Eats small fish, crabs, shrimp, octopuses, fat worms, even rays!

"Excuse me," I said, holding up my notebook as everyone looked at me. Even the cameras swung around to face me. "But why are there two animals called leopard sharks if they are two different animals?"

"She's smart." Dr. Chandrika smiled. "Can I see your notebook and what you have written?" I handed her my messy writing and she made approving noises as she looked over my notes. She looked up at me and motioned for me to follow her, which I did, cameras trailing behind us. Out of the corner of my eye, I spotted Mr. Savage whispering something to Mark as he fiddled with his camera.

"So 'leopard shark' is a common name, or what people outside science call these animals. Many animals, like these two, have multiple common names. Sometimes they share the same common name," she said as we turned down the hall into a giant, dark room.

She flipped the switch, and the place came to life, showing that one wall was made of glass. Suddenly, we were transported to an underwater coral forest. Algae and branching coral swayed in the currents, with brightly colored fish schooling above the creamy, sandy bottom. I spotted a stingray swimming lazily around.

Then I saw them. The leopard sharks! Or zebra sharks? They kind of looked half zebra and half leopard.

"Oh!" I said, surprised by seeing the animals . . . and that I didn't know animals could go by so many names.

"The name you have written next to their common name? That starts with an S? That's what we call the scientific name. Each animal has their own unique scientific name. No two are alike. So that is what we use when referring to these animals." Dr. Chandrika pointed to the leopard sharks. "These

STINGRAY

- Stingrays are common throughout the world, in tropical or sub-tropical waters.

- There are over two hundred different stingray species.

- These creatures have no real bones in their entire body. Their skeleton is formed by cartilage, a flexible connective tissue.

- Their diet is typically composed of food like snails, small fish, clams, and crustaceans.

are the leopard sharks scientifically known as *Stegostoma tigrinum*. Make sense?" she asked. I nodded and thanked her for explaining that.

My parents and Feye, who had followed us into the massive room, all let out audible gasps at seeing the giant aquarium. Feye quickly took his phone out for a picture, snapping multiple shots of the resting sharks. As the adults went back to talking among themselves, Feye came closer to me.

"Think we could swim with them? The tank looks big enough," he said.

"Oh, you can actually give it a try if you want," Dr. Chandrika said. "We've got some spare goggles, snorkels, and fins."

I looked up at my parents. "Oh, can we? Please?!" I was ready to do anything to make sure I ended up in that tank. Fortunately, Mr. Savage was on my side.

"I think it's a great idea! We can film the kids

swimming with the sharks. We'll see the fearless Villalobos kids face these dangerous animals!" Mr. Savage cried.

"Do you guys even have swimsuits with you?" Dad asked, raising his eyebrows.

"Uh, yeah. I learned my lesson." I yanked at my shirt to show my black swimsuit underneath. Not that I knew today we would be swimming with leopard sharks in a tank . . . but a girl should always be prepared!

I looked into the tank, watching as one of the sharks rose from the sandy bottom and began to swim toward us, floating through the water with ease. That powerful tail swished from side to side effortlessly. Sharks are incredible creatures. They've been around longer than trees and evolved for millions of years. This was just one of their thousands of final forms.

"Earth to A!" I heard Feye say as I brought myself back to the present.

I gave them a shy smile. "Sorry, I was just thinking about how much I love sharks."

Dr. Chandrika returned my smile. "Then it's a good thing we just decided to let you go in with them!"

I let out a whoop and, before anyone could stop me, took my clothes off to reveal my swimsuit beneath.

"Someone sure is excited." Feye laughed. Everyone laughed with him as I dashed to the box of snorkels and masks nearby.

While we got ready to go in, the adults talked about what shots to take for the cameras, and pretty soon it was time to dive on in!

"Remember, slow and steady strokes and don't make any sudden movements that could scare them off. No touching them, okay?" Dr. Chandrika instructed as she came to the top of the aquarium with us. We waved to our parents below and blew them a kiss before jumping into the warm water.

And in we went! As the bubbles cleared from our initial jump in, I suddenly was surrounded by colorful fish and towering coral. The sharks, having heard us enter, swam underneath one of the structures to hide.

"It's okay! We aren't here to hurt you!" I said through my snorkel.

Feye pointed up, signaling for us to surface. When we popped up above the surface, he shook his head at me. "Don't scream at them; you're gonna scare them!" he said.

Oops. I forgot that part. *Dial down the excitement, A.*

We went back down, me trying to free dive like Zev. I was sort of getting the hang of it, even making my way down to the bottom of the tank near the sharks! They stayed under the coral but didn't seem as terrified as before.

I completely lost track of time, too focused on my brother and trying to perfect my free diving, and I was startled when Mr. Savage tapped on the glass and pointed to his watch. Time was up.

"Thank you, sharks!" I said into the water, waving at them as we popped back up.

"Have fun?" Dr. Chandrika asked.

I nodded. "Oh heck yeah, I did!"

CHAPTER SIXTEEN

After my swim with the leopard sharks, Dr. Chandrika, my family, and I spent a few days meeting up regularly to "iron out the details" about the Shark Appreciation Festival. It's a lot of work to bring something like this to life in such a super-short amount of time, but we had all done it! Finally, today was the day. I couldn't wait to start sharing my love of sharks with a whole new audience.

"Well, what do you guys think?" Mr. Savage said as we came closer to the beach where we were holding the festival. Brightly colored lanterns hung from the lush green trees and a banner in multiple languages was posted near the entrance to the fish market entrance. In English, it said *WILD SURVIVAL!* SHARK APPRECIATION FESTIVAL. Tables had been set up with different activities: Some had shark coloring pages, at others you could make your own shark bookmark, and one even had trivia where if you got questions right, you could win squishy shark toys. The beach was full of locals, laughing, chatting, and looking through everything.

I breathed a sigh of relief. People had actually showed up!

When we got to the market building, I peeked inside, where a stage had been set up, along with my photo gallery. Mr. Savage and the network had paid all the fishers to allow us to use the market space for talks by the local shark scientists.

"Happy?" Mom whispered into my ear, hugging me tightly. I nodded, tears in my eyes as I took in everything. I could see the photos that I had taken of the sharks found in the markets hung up next to those that Mark and Alice had taken of the same kinds of sharks, but alive and vivid in the ocean. Below each photo, I spied the captions I had written out about the beauty of the species and why they were so important . . . and then the translation written by Mr. Manil below. Tiger sharks, whale sharks, hammerheads . . . they were heartbreakingly beautiful. Yes, yes, I was happy. I was *realmente emocionada*.

"Holy cannoli," Feye whispered, looking around at the festival's setup and taking his phone out of the waterproof case he had it in to snap a picture. He knew I only got this super excited about sharks, tacos, and puppies.

"Time to get this party started!" Mr. Savage said as he walked away from us and toward the stage. From behind the stage, I could see the "The Ocean and I" photo gallery! This was the gallery Dr. Chandrika had helped set up, where she and Alice

had gone around taking photos and doing inter-
views with the local fishermen. I was so excited to
read all their stories.

> *"I'm a fifth-generation fisherman. We*
> *are thankful the ocean provides us jobs*
> *and food."*
> *"My father taught me how to fish. We*
> *can't imagine doing anything else. Our*
> *respect for the ocean runs deep."*
> *"The ocean gives us everything we need.*
> *We need to protect her!"*

Taking the microphone out of its stand, Mr.
Savage held it up to his mouth and tapped it once,
twice. "Testing, testing, can everyone hear me?"
After seeing nods from around the venue, he con-
tinued. "Welcome, everybody, to the *Wild Survival!*
Shark Appreciation Festival hosted by the Villalobos

family, who is here right now!" Mr. Savage said. He motioned for us to come up and join him onstage, and I thought we must have looked cute in our matching khaki zoo outfits. "This is Julio and Evelyn and their kids, Feye and Adrianna. You may have seen Adrianna and Feye around here already."

We waved as Mr. Savage introduced us. From the stage, I could see all my friends had made it. I was so happy Zev, Dilip, Punya, and Manisha had all come.

"We have a day jam-packed with *jawsome* fun, so make sure to check out our tables of activities, the photo gallery, and the talks that will happen throughout the day," Mr. Savage added. "I hope you brought your swimsuits and some snorkels, too, because we are having a community-wide snorkel trip out to the beach to see if we can spot some sharks! No snorkel? No problem! We have lots of extra masks for those who forgot or don't have them! So go, enjoy! The snorkel will begin in a few hours."

Mr. Savage put the microphone back on its stand and a translator took his place, reiterating what he had said and inviting the first speaker of the day to come up to the stage.

"So, what do we do now?" Mom asked.

"You go have fun! Kids, here are your 'Villalobos Vision' GoPros, and Mark and Alice will follow all four of you randomly as you have fun! Mingle!" Mr. Savage said, handing Feye and me the cameras. "But first I need to talk about the epic monster snorkel shot."

"Monster snorkel shot?" Feye asked.

"You know, the 'Civilians swim with terrifying beasts of the sea.' Having you guys among these killer sharks is going to be a killer shot!" Mr. Savage said.

"Rick, the entire point of this was to *appreciate* sharks, not vilify them. They get that enough," Dad said.

"Well, so long as none of the sharks bite people,

they won't get vilified." Mr. Savage shrugged. He then looked at me. "Try not to get bitten by one, okay?" He winked and left to go talk to Mark and Alice.

After going to each table as a family, I sat down and watched one of the expert speakers the network had brought in. As I listened to him, I was struck by how passionate he was about the topic of shark finning. He showed slides about what the practice was, talked about how many dried shark fins had recently been tested around the world for toxins like mercury, and how many had a super-high level, on average six to ten times higher than what a safe level would be.

At the end of his talk, everyone clapped and waited for the announcer to introduce the next speaker—Dr. Chandrika! She scanned the crowd as she introduced herself as the CEO of Waves of Action, the Sri Lankan organization based on marine science education and advocacy that was helping host the festival.

I'm not sure how I didn't spot him before, but a cough made me look down my row to see Mr. Savage only a few feet away from me. "Mr. Savage!" I whispered, motioning for him to come closer to me. Dr. Chandrika continued to explain how her talk was going to be about how our seafood choices impact sharks in ways we wouldn't think.

"Yes, Adrianna?" Mr. Savage asked.

"Are we recording Dr. Chandrika?" I motioned, pointing up at Dr. Chandrika, hoping she got a ton of airtime on this show.

"Of course. Her organization donated a lot of the time and resources, and she was instrumental in making sure we had this *fintastic* lineup of interesting speakers," Mr. Savage explained.

After that, Mr. Savage and I stayed quiet and listened to the talk, which was fascinating and had me downloading every sustainable seafood app on my phone ... just in case I needed one and it wasn't available in some part of the world we traveled to. In the middle of it, Mr. Savage left my side to instruct Mark to get some different angles of Dr. Chandrika, taking pictures of her with his own phone while she discussed her work with ocean plastic pollution and Sri Lankan blue whales. As her presentation came to an end, Feye suggested we head outside to get a snack.

I waved goodbye to Dr. Chandrika and went outside to sample some of the different foods being dished out. Then Feye and I joined Zev, Manisha, Dilip, and Punya in listening to a live band and dancing. It wasn't long before we all were sweaty thanks to the humidity and sun.

"Adrianna! Feye!" we heard our mother call. She waved at us to come over to where she was, near the water. She, Alice, and Mark were all suited up for the community snorkel, which would be the closing event of our festival. *It's go time!*

"It's time for the snorkel. Are you coming with

us?" I asked my friends. Manisha and Dilip looked at Punya, who shook her head. "I don't know how to swim. Nobody in my family does," she said.

I saw Zev look around for something. He dashed off before quickly returning with a life jacket and something that looked like an old flotation pool noodle that had seen better days. "You and I can just dip our feet in for now," he said. "We'll go together while Adrianna and Feye go work."

Punya smiled and nodded. Feye and I ran across the hot sand to meet our parents. Mr. Savage now had a megaphone in his hand. Not that he needed one because he was so loud!

"Alright, everyone! We're about to go into the water!" he shouted, the megaphone giving off some feedback and letting out a loud wailing noise that made everyone cover their ears with their hands.

"Okay, let's try this again. We're about to go into the water. For those who don't have snorkels, feel free to borrow some we have up here, but please share so everyone who wants a turn can have one!" Mr. Savage said. "But first, here are some safety rules to keep in mind while swimming near sharks." He passed the microphone to my dad, who thanked Mr. Savage and then welcomed everyone once again.

"As you can see, we have lifeguards here! They will not only be making sure we swim safely but they are also on the lookout for any dangerous situations. If any of them blow a whistle, please get out of the water in a calm manner," Dad directed. "Next, please stick with the group. Stay on *this* side of the shark net and don't poke your fingers out."

We had a mesh net set up for there to be an area where no sharks would be able to get through so we could enjoy the sharks while staying safe.

Dad let the local translator relay his message, and then he continued. "If you see a large school of fish, please do not swim by it, as that can become a valuable feeding opportunity for the sharks! Keep your distance from any bleeding animals, and if you see a shark feeding, please give it some space.

"Please do not try to touch, kiss, or ride any sharks. These are wild animals and they will defend themselves—usually by biting! Give them plenty of space so they do not feel threatened and lash out. And finally, if you are feeling uneasy, do not push yourself! Get out of the water and enjoy the view because, if you are forcing yourself to do this, you won't enjoy it anyway."

As Dad spoke to the crowd and Mr. Savage swapped instructions with the lifeguards, my eyes wandered among the unfamiliar faces in the crowd that was huddled near us in anticipation of going into the water. Would this many people scare off the sharks? I let my thoughts wander off until I spotted one . . . two . . . three familiar faces!

"Mamá, mira," I said, tugging on her arm. She

followed my gaze and smiled, gripping my dad's hand and squeezing it, nodding in the direction of the trio that had showed up.

Mr. and Mrs. Gamage were off to one side of the crowd, between them a frail-looking man who needed assistance standing up. He couldn't have been much older than Mr. Gamage, and as I looked down at his leg, I could see why he was having trouble standing on the uneven sand. Against his dark skin were bright pink scars, gnarled around his leg from his foot to at least his knee. His face was slightly grimaced, as if he was in pain, but he had a set determination in his eyes.

With Mr. Savage done talking, and the rest of the crowd starting to either dive into the water or sift through the pile of life jackets and snorkels available on the beach, I tugged on my mom's arm again. As a family, we all went up to greet the Gamages.

"It is so nice to see you, Mr. and Mrs. Gamage.

You must be Mr. Gamage's brother we have heard so much about," my mom said, extending her hand to shake their hands. The man nodded, and the Gamages introduced us. Mr. Manil came up from behind us and said hello as well, shaking Mr. Gamage's hand and bowing to his wife and his brother.

"Thank you for coming," my dad said. "We know it must not be easy to be here, maybe even scary."

Mr. Manil translated, and the man nodded again, then looked straight at me. He said something to Mr. Manil while continuing to look at me, and when he stopped, we all looked to Mr. Manil.

"He wants to know if you're the young girl bitten by the crocodile," Mr. Manil said.

I looked at the brother and nodded, extending my leg so he could see my purplish scars. He released Mr. and Mrs. Gamage to bend down and look closer, and then he extended out his leg next to mine.

As the brother spoke, Mr. Manil translated. "He

says he wants to thank you for having the courage to speak out for animals that do not have a voice. That although he is still scared of what happened, he is inspired by your bravery and is even thinking of going close to the water today."

"It's the first time he's said that." Mr. Gamage said, looking surprised.

"That's really cool." Feye beamed.

Smiling, I held out my hand to Mr. Gamage's brother, who hesitatingly took it.

"We'll face this fear together," I said. We all turned toward the calm blue water. Already there were large groups in the water, swimming past the coral heads that Feye, Dilip, and I had visited on the day I rescued the turtle.

At the water's edge, Zev, Dilip, and Manisha all huddled around Punya. She eased into the water until she was about waist deep. I saw Zev mimicking swimming motions for Punya to practice.

Before long, Mr. Gamage's brother and I were at the water's edge. I heard Mr. Savage wave one of the camera operators our way. "What a great moment! Two survivors taking a dip to brave our ocean's fiercest predators!"

I just tuned him out. From the corner of my eye, I could see Alice's camera focus in on us as we got our feet wet. Mr. Gamage's brother started laughing and splashed his feet a little.

"Thank you," Mr. Gamage said through Mr. Manil as they joined us. Mr. Gamage grabbed his brother's hand. "I've got him. Go ahead out to play with your friends."

I smiled and waved, then plunged into the water. Feye had gone into the water ahead of me, away from the shark net, and I swam to meet him.

"There's a lot to see today!" Feye called out, before ducking his head back underneath the water.

I put my head underwater and was delighted

to see so much life beneath us. Fish of many colors surrounded us, just like they had in the waters of Pigeon Island National Park. A sea turtle swam by lazily and nestled itself in between some patches of coral to rest.

"Incoming!" Feye said. One . . . two . . . three sharks came from our left and dove sharply into the brightly colored coral looking for food.

With most of the fish scattering into areas too hard to reach for the blacktip reef sharks, the predators had slowed down to a slow cruising speed. The sunlight glinted off them, and patterns from the sun danced on the sharks' cream-colored skin. They looked peaceful now, flying effortlessly through the water.

I came up to the surface and swam back to the shore. The Gamage brothers still stood at the shoreline, their feet in the ocean.

I waved again, but I saw looks of concern flash

across their faces. Then a scream cut through the air. All around me, people were quickly swimming back to the sand and getting out of the water.

"What are they yelling, Mr. Manil?" I asked, climbing out of the water myself.

"'Monster. Huge man-eating monster coming' is what I just heard someone say," Mr. Manil answered.

"Monster?" I asked. My parents and Feye were still in the water and didn't look concerned. I trusted their take on the situation, so I waded back in and swam out to meet them. I ducked my head underwater to see if I could see what had startled everyone back to shore.

Something was definitely coming our way... something BIG.

CHAPTER SEVENTEEN

The water, now murky from the number of people who had frantically swum closer to shore, made it hard to see exactly what was coming our way. But whatever it was, it was huge! A monster, though? I wasn't so sure.

"Can you see anything?" Feye called out.

"*¡Hijos! ¡Con cuidado!* Be careful!" Dad said, trying to keep his head above the waves while he treaded water.

I squinted, trying to see if I could make out the outline of the huge animal. Sure enough, it looked like a big fish with two huge side fins. I only knew of one fish that could be this big. I swam closer toward the animal, which I noticed was also very close to the surface. It gave me an idea.

That must mean a dorsal fin should be sticking out of the water!

"I think I know what it is!" I said as my head popped out of the water. My family, who were still with their faces underwater, joined me at the surface.

"There's no mistaking that fin!" I exclaimed, pointing out the blue fin that was covered in what looked like constellations.

"Mr. Manil! Tell them it isn't a dangerous shark!" I yelled back to shore. "It's just a whale shark! They're harmless!"

I could see that Mr. Manil and Dr. Chandrika were trying to explain that the whale shark was harmless, but people seemed to be drifting away from the beach entirely. This couldn't be how the festival ended! There had to be something we could do.

WHALE SHARK

- Whale sharks are actually a giant species of fish. They can grow up to about 40 feet long (12 meters).

- These animals are filter feeders. Like whales, they don't bite food, but feed by drawing in water through their mouths. With the water comes smaller organisms like plankton, fish, or squid.

- All whale sharks have a distinct pattern of white dots on their backs that can be used to identify individuals, much like the human fingerprint.

- The average life span of a whale shark is seventy years.

I locked eyes with Dr. Chandrika, who took off her outfit to reveal a swimsuit underneath. She dove dramatically and swam out into the water to demonstrate it was safe to stay.

"It's okay, everyone! It's a whale shark!" Dr. Chandrika announced to everyone on the shore. "Whale sharks are filter feeders and mostly eat tiny plankton!"

Mr. Manil translated for us as Dr. Chandrika continued to tell everyone that whale sharks were harmless and that this was an exciting opportunity to see an incredible creature—some might even consider it good luck!

Some people on the beach laughed. Realizing there really was no danger, they relaxed and made their way back into the warm water. The whale shark, unaware it had caused such a commotion, continued to flick its enormous tail back and forth as it swam away from us. At first it was just our small group with the whale shark, but after a few minutes it felt like everybody who had attended the festival was out in the water wanting to get a glimpse of this gentle giant. Many yelped as they took in its huge size but were soon mesmerized by the way it glided through the water.

"Say cheese!" Feye said, holding up the "Villalobos Vision" camera to take a selfie of us and the disappearing whale shark behind us. I noticed two things in that moment. First, the fear on everyone's faces around us had been replaced by awe. It was a wonderful feeling, knowing we had helped change at least a few minds about this particular shark species. I would have normally been over the moon about that, except the second thing I noticed put a pit in my stomach.

There, on the beach, stood a familiar blonde woman and man with a black hat. "It's the poachers,"

I whispered, not realizing I had said it out loud. Who else would be in an all-black ensemble on the beach? It was them; I just knew it. There was no denying it. Had they heard a rumor that we might be releasing the Pondicherry shark back into the wild? I had to go check on that shark!

Quickly I waded out of the water and over to the Gamages and Mr. Manil. "Mr. Manil," I said. "Will you ask the Gamages if their store is open? I, uh, have to use the bathroom. And I don't want to use one of the portable toilets." It was a lame excuse, but it would have to do.

"Sure, no problem," he said through Mr. Manil. "The side door is unlocked."

As I threw on my clothes and started down the beach, my mother called to ask where I was going.

"Oh, Adrianna is just going to use the bathroom at Mr. Gamage's restaurant," Feye said. I hadn't realized he'd been close enough to hear my exchange. He looked straight at me as he said it, and I wondered if he knew I was lying. I mouthed "thank you" at him and then threw clothes over my wet swimsuit.

You need proof it is the poachers, Adrianna.

Right . . . proof . . . proof . . . my camera! I grabbed the backpack my parents had packed for us filled with sunscreen, sunglasses, hats, snacks, and more. I had left my phone at the hotel but had tucked my camera in with my stuff to take pictures of the festival. I'd been having so much fun, I'd completely forgotten about it until now. I looped it around my neck and started to jog to the restaurant. My soggy shirt and pants felt funny, but I tried to pick up my pace.

Faster, Adrianna! Faster!

My legs, tired from swimming and running, gave in for a second. Before I knew it, I was on the ground, my knees and palms skinned from the rough dirt and gravel below. "Dang it . . ." I muttered, biting back tears that threatened to spill over my hot face.

I took a deep breath and dusted myself off. As I looked up, the pain in my hands was replaced by a pang in my stomach. The door to the Gamages' restaurant was standing open. A brick had been left in the doorframe. That didn't seem right. Slowly, I walked close enough to the restaurant to peek inside.

There, I saw the blonde woman standing on top of a chair, bent over the tank, her arms in the water. The man with the black hat stood next to her. At his feet, a tank filled with water rested on a metal cart. They presumably planned to transport the shark in there until they got . . . well, wherever they were going with it.

Think fast, Adrianna! I looked down at my camera and decided to take a picture of them in the act of stealing the shark. Surely with me being able to describe them and this photo, they would get caught before they got too far.

Quietly, I slipped through the restaurant's door. I bent down to wedge myself under a table. As I got into a good position, I took a deep breath and turned the camera on. Focusing, I made sure to get both of them in the frame before my finger put pressure on the button.

Click!

Flash!

Oh no! I really needed to learn how to turn the flash off!

The woman, who had managed to capture the Pondicherry shark in her hands, quickly dropped it back into its original tank with a splash, and spun around to see me. "It's that girl!" she said, pointing at me with a dripping finger. The man placed the tank he was holding down on a nearby table as he lunged toward me, missing my ankle by just a few inches as I tried to scramble out from underneath the table.

The camera! I can't let them get the camera! I looked around, trying to find somewhere to hide it. *Think, A! Think!*

I quickly took the camera's neck strap off and threw the piece of technology across the floor, away from all of us. I hoped it wouldn't slam against the concrete wall. Otherwise, it would surely shatter into a million pieces. Bye-bye to my grandmother's gift—and my evidence! Thankfully, I didn't have to worry about that because it slowed to a stop before it hit the wall.

Before I knew it, each poacher had one of my arms in their hands and the man let out a curse word I *know* would end up with a bit of money in the curse word jar back at home.

"Let go of me!" I said, anger bubbling from deep

within me and tingeing my vision with red. I struggled and knocked the man's sunglasses off his face.

"You! You have been a thorn in our side for these last two jobs we've had," the man said in his thick Irish accent. A scowl darkened his face, and I scowled right back, wondering where this bravery was coming from.

"Adrianna!" I heard my name being called from outside. From inside the restaurant we could all see Feye making his way toward us.

The two poachers exchanged a look and dropped my arms. "This isn't over!" the man spat at me. They turned and ran for the back of the restaurant.

CHAPTER EIGHTEEN

"Adrianna?" Feye said again from the door. He poked his head in.

"What is going on?" he asked. "Did you really just need to use the bathroom?"

"Feye!" I yelled, running toward him. I gave him a big hug. The tears I had bottled up while facing the poachers suddenly burst through the dam, pouring down my cheeks.

"What happened?!" he asked, his voice full of concern.

I pointed to the camera, my other arm still

wrapped around my brother. "Get that and I'll explain everything."

Feye let me go and retrieved my camera. I quickly took it and looked it over to see if it was damaged from my throw. Thankfully, it seemed okay.

I turned the camera on and started flipping through the photo gallery. But when I got to the last photo, I didn't see a shark theft in progress; all I saw was a black rectangle. *Oh no.*

"What?" I whispered, staring at the blank photo in disbelief. And then I turned the camera around to see that the lens cap was still firmly in place.

You didn't take it off before taking the photo. Again.

I smacked my head with my free hand.

"A? Tell me what's going on! I'm getting worried here," Feye said.

"How long have I been gone?" I asked, looking up at my brother.

"Like ten minutes?" Feye shrugged. "I could tell

you lied to Mom about why you wanted to come to the restaurant, so I wanted to see what the real reason was. Plus, I had some good news."

"What's the good news?" I asked.

"First tell me what's going on." He motioned to the extra tank left behind by the poachers. His eyes narrowed. "Were you trying to steal the shark?"

"What? Feye, no!" I said. I was no thief!

"So then what's the story?" he asked.

"You won't believe me. I have no proof," I whispered, putting the camera down with a sad thud.

"Try me."

I told Feye about seeing the poachers on the beach and then how they'd confronted me after my camera flash went off.

"We have to tell the police," he said when I finished.

"Tell them what? I have no proof. And Mom and Dad will be furious."

Feye looked thoughtful. "I guess you're right. Even though I think we should. But they might just get really mad. We can't have you getting kicked off the show again!"

Suddenly, my head shot up. Maybe we did have evidence.

I looked around and ... bingo! The sunglasses I had knocked off! The poacher had never retrieved them.

I grabbed them and held them up. "Feye, look! His sunglasses! It's proof."

"Proof of what? Those could belong to anyone," Feye answered.

"Maybe we can give them to the police and they can swab them for DNA and find the poacher," I offered.

Feye shook his head. "You've been watching too much TV. That's not how it works."

"But it's something." I held them up to look at them.

Besides the odd logo we had seen on their clothing before, nothing else stood out about the sunglasses.

"I guess." Feye shrugged. "I don't know what it's going to prove, though."

We stood in silence for a second.

"Isn't it a weird coincidence that we just saw them in Cuba, and now they're here?" I asked.

Feye had no answer.

We looked around us. "We better clean up," I said, searching for something to sop up the spilled tank water.

"Oh! Wait! My good news!" Feye said as he looked out the restaurant's glass door. "We could use the tank, actually."

I looked at my brother in confusion. "What? Why?"

"The Gamage family agreed to release the shark back into the wild! And put new fish in the old tank!" he said.

"What?!" I squealed. "Really?"

"Oh, they're coming now. Look," Feye said, bringing me to the door and waving at our parents, the Gamage family, and the camera crew. Mr. Savage led the way toward us.

"Wow, what made them change their minds?" I asked Feye.

"You did, of course. And their time at the shark festival today. They got to see some blacktip reef sharks up close after you left," Feye said, pulling out his phone.

He showed me a video of the water's surface full of beautiful fins. They swam in a mesmerizing synchronized fashion. Wow. I wish I had been there to see them in person.

"I livestreamed it to my followers." Feye winked as the group entered the restaurant.

"Oh! Hello, Adrianna and Feye!" Mr. Savage said, his eyebrows sort of furrowed in surprise and confusion at seeing the two of us standing in front of the shark tank. "You got a tank out and filled it for the shark!"

"Yeah," Feye started. "Adrianna was just *so* excited to hear about the Gamages reconsidering. We found the cart out back."

I nodded in agreement with my brother. "Lucky find!" I couldn't help adding. But my parents were so happy about the Gamages that they didn't seem to register anything odd about that.

"Oh, of course you were excited." Mom beamed. "Our Mother of Sharks!"

Mr. Savage clapped his hands and started belting out instructions. "Alright. Lights, camera, action! Let's film the family getting this shark into a tank to transport it out into the wild!"

CHAPTER NINETEEN

Mr. Savage ran around the restaurant trying to get the perfect light on my mom and dad as they transferred the Pondicherry shark from one tank into another.

I needed to free up my hands in case they needed help, but didn't want to forget my camera or the sunglasses. "Hey, Mr. Savage, can Feye and I put some stuff in your bag?" I asked, spotting his black duffel on one of the tables.

He nodded. "Sure, kid. There should be a dry bag in there—put your things in there and don't get my stuff wet and dirty!" Off he went to bark more orders.

Feye tossed me his phone to put in the bag. I unzipped it and opened up the bright yellow dry bag. We used these waterproof bags all the time for protecting stuff that couldn't get wet, like phones or other equipment. I fished in my pocket for the poacher's glasses. Except . . . wait, had I already dropped them in the bag?

Peering into Mr. Savage's dry bag, I almost did a double take. The glasses in my pocket and the glasses in the bag were exactly the same! Identical logo and everything. Making sure no one was looking at me too closely, I peeked at the other stuff in the bag. There was a plain black shirt with the same logo, albeit faded.

"Adrianna! Hurry up and get to your spot," Dad said. I nodded at him, put my camera and Feye's phone in the bag, and quickly closed everything up. The glasses would be safer in my pocket for now.

I took my place near the front doors, still reeling from seeing the identical stuff as the poachers' in Mr. Savage's bag. What did that mean? I'd never seen that logo anywhere else before, but maybe they just shopped at the same online stores? But it was definitely weird that the poachers had now shown up at two of our filming locations. I stared at the back of Mr. Savage's head. He seemed surprised when he walked into the restaurant earlier. Why?

I knew I had to put this new discovery aside for now and focus on releasing the shark, but my hands wouldn't stop shaking.

"Mark, to the left, Alice, to the right. Connor, does everyone have microphones?" Mr. Savage asked. His voice cut through my thoughts and brought me back to the present.

"Done, boss! They're good to go," Connor said.

He stood up, slung his sound bag over one of his shoulders, and plopped his headphones around his ears, giving us a thumbs-up.

"And . . . action!"

As my dad narrated why my mom was trying to get the shark out of the tank, I watched as her hands held steady over the water's surface. For a few minutes there was silence, the only noise coming from the shark thrashing away from my mother's grasp as her hands darted into the water to grab it.

"*¡Lo tengo!* Got it!" Mom said as she held the shark up to transfer it over. Third time was the charm! Dad held up the tank so my mom could slip the shark into the water.

"Tell me you got that!" Mr. Savage said.

"Got it!" Alice and Mark both replied.

"Let's get going. We want this shark out into the ocean before it runs out of oxygen," my mom said, looking down at the small tank. The gray shark swished back and forth as my parents carried the small aquarium out of the restaurant and put it in the back of a golf cart.

"See if you can get some footage of them going to the beach with the shark!" Mr. Savage yelled.

I turned around to make sure Mr. Gamage shut the restaurant door behind him. He saw me looking and smiled. I returned the smile and nodded in thanks.

As we neared the beach, we could see a crowd had gathered to watch the shark release. We parked and Mr. Manil helped us organize the shark festival—goers into a long line. One by one, everyone would help pass the tank from the parking lot to the water's edge.

"Tell me you're getting this, you guys," Mr. Savage muttered. Alice and Mark nodded, their cameras up on their shoulders, letting us know they were rolling by the bright red blinking lights that went off every few seconds.

We watched as my mom and dad gently picked up the tank off the back of the golf cart and passed it to the first waiting couple. They took a second to admire the thrashing gray animal and said a few words over the shark. This went on for a few more couples before I turned to Mr. Manil.

"Mr. Manil, what are they saying?" I asked, curious.

He smiled at me. "Let's go closer!" he said. The next two people to take the shark tank were Zev and Manisha. I could see them struggling a little bit, their arms shaking as they each said something to the shark.

Mr. Manil asked them if they were willing to share what parting words they had said to the shark as they passed the heavy tank on to Punya and Dilip.

"We're thanking the shark for teaching us not to judge an animal by how scary it looks," Zev explained, flashing me a megawatt smile.

"And we're wishing it a safe journey out there in the big, wide world!" Manisha added, laughing.

"I told it that it always has a home in our waters," Punya said, after she and Dilip had passed the tank along to the next pair of volunteers.

"And we're telling the shark to tell its friends to come visit! It was awesome seeing all those sharks today—we want to see more like that!" Dilip finished.

"Adrianna, why are you crying? Can you tell the camera?" Mr. Savage asked.

I wiped the tears away with the back of my hand and then rubbed my hands against my pants.

"It's just . . . a beautiful thought. That people would care so much about an animal they used to be scared of . . . it just gives me hope," I explained.

I felt my heart hammer in my chest, hoping I wasn't messing up how I was saying this. "I'm just really happy," I said.

I watched silently as the shark continued to be passed down from caring hands to caring hands, waiting to be taken by my mom and dad, who were now at the water's edge.

Mom motioned for me to come meet them. "We think you and Feye should be the ones to release the shark," Mom said, eyeing the tank, now just a few people away from us.

When they took the shark from the other people, they passed it on to us. I could see the blinking red lights of the cameras and could tell by Mr. Savage's expression that he wanted us to say something.

I looked down at the shark and whispered, "Safe travels, *tiburón*. And no matter what anyone says, you are no monster."

Feye smiled down at the shark and said, "See ya later, shark! Go rule those oceans!"

And with that, we walked into the water until it was splashing against our shins. Once there, we tipped the tank over and the shark slid into the ocean. I wondered how long it had been since it had seen the waves . . . would it know how to survive? Judging by how quickly it zipped away, I thought it was going to be just fine!

As everyone gathered at the edge of the water, waiting for us to set the shark free, they cheered when they spotted it swimming away from the shore into deeper water.

"Goodbye, shark!" "*¡Adiós!*" "*Ayubowan!*"

I looked back to see everyone waving good-bye, some waving their wet shirts and snorkels in the air as they bid the shark safe travels, wherever it went.

"And cut! That's a wrap, Villalobos family!" Mr.

Savage said triumphantly. He looked as if he wanted to say more, but at that precise moment his phone started ringing. Holding up a finger, he stepped away from the noise of the loud crowd.

I turned to the Gamage family, smiling warmly at them. "Thank you for having such an open mind about sharks and their importance," I said. Mr. Manil translated for me.

Mr. Gamage bowed his head. "Thank you for your bravery," he said through Mr. Manil.

I nodded and looked behind him as my friends came toward us to say goodbye. Excusing myself, I jogged over to them and gave them each a hug. "I can't thank you guys enough for showing me how beautiful Sri Lanka is," I started. "Zev, Manisha, Punya, Dilip . . . I'm going to miss you. Promise to stay in touch?"

Zev held up his phone as he said he would have his people call my people, and everyone laughed.

Turning to him, I gave him another hug as I thanked him for blindly going on adventures with me.

"It was fun. There's definitely no one like Adrianna Villalobos in the world, that's for sure!" Zev said. "You are one of a kind! And I'll never forget you." My new friends nodded.

I blushed. That was the nicest thing any guy had ever said to me, besides my family. What could I even say to that? I opened my mouth to say something when a shrill voice rang over the noise. "*Familia* Villalobos!" Mr. Savage called, interrupting our conversation and waving us over with urgency. "I need to talk to you, *pronto*!"

"We'll talk more soon, *amigos*!" I said as our family went to Mr. Savage to see what the important news was.

"What is it, Rick?" Dad asked.

"We just got our next assignment!"

"Any guesses?" Mom asked us.

"Alaska!" Feye said. We all looked at him with a raised eyebrow. *Alaska? Where did that come from?*

"What? They have . . . bears," offered Feye.

"South Africa?" I asked, crossing my fingers to return back to the African continent.

Mr. Savage shook his head.

"Get ready, gang," Mr. Savage said, holding up the e-mail that had just come through. "We're going to Mexico . . . to film some jaguars."

AUTHOR'S NOTE

I have always been fascinated by misunderstood predators, and to me, sharks are one of the most misunderstood. The first time I ever saw a shark on-screen was during Discovery Channel's "Shark Week," where I watched a great white shark (*Carcharodon carcharias*) breaching out of the water and into the air. It was chasing a seal and, at the same time, stealing my heart.

The first time I saw a shark in the wild was when I was training for my scuba diving license in the British Virgin Islands. This trip would cement whether or not I *really* wanted to become a marine biologist. It was here that I came across a nurse shark (*Ginglymostoma cirratum*) and screamed into my regulator: *Finally! A wild shark!*

Since then, I have dedicated my life to learning all about sharks and their relatives (skates, rays, and chimaeras). But I am also passionate about teaching people around me about these beautiful animals, the threats they face, and how we can all protect them. I still get just as excited when seeing sharks as I did the first day I came across that nurse shark. How lucky I am to live in a world and a time when there are so many different species! Even as a shark scientist, I am constantly learning new things about sharks—I love being a "forever student" of these amazing creatures.

No two days are the same for me. Some days I am out in the field from before the sunrise to long after the moon takes its place. I love the smells of sunscreen, frozen fish, stinky bait, and salty ocean air equally! Other weeks I am behind a computer screen for days at a time, analyzing the data I recovered from the field, writing up reports, and publishing papers. I love the variety of it all.

My research has shown me that for a healthy

ocean, we need a healthy shark population. So, we should not be afraid of an ocean full of sharks . . . we should be afraid of an ocean without them. I hope this book sparked awe and wonder, not fear. It would be amazing if it made you see sharks in a different light! Who knows, maybe one day you will be a fellow shark researcher.

COMMONLY ASKED QUESTIONS ABOUT SHARKS

HOW MANY SHARK SPECIES ARE THERE?

There are over five hundred different shark species that have been found so far . . . and counting!

WHERE CAN YOU FIND SHARKS?

All over the world! Sharks are found in salt water (the ocean), brackish water (a mixture of salt water and freshwater), and freshwater (e.g., rivers).

WHAT DO SHARKS EAT?

It depends on the species. Some common prey items are fish, marine mammals, birds, sea turtles, and even other sharks.

WHAT IS THE BIGGEST SHARK?

The whale shark (*Rhincodon typus*) usually grows to 39 feet (12 meters) in length, although a fully grown whale shark can reach up to an incredible 65 feet (20 meters) long. The largest confirmed individual had a length of 62 feet (18.8 meters). Found throughout the world's tropical and warm, temperate seas, it gets its name from its large size (as big as whales)!

I'VE HEARD ABOUT MEGALODON—IS IT REAL?

Megalodon (scientifically known as *Otodus megalodon* but was previously *Carcharodon* or *Carcharocles megalodon*) is a gigantic shark that lived nearly worldwide in tropical-temperate regions up until around 2.6 million years ago. It is known almost exclusively from fossilized teeth and is regarded as one of the largest carnivores, if not superpredators, that have ever lived on Earth.

WHAT ARE THE BIGGEST THREATS TO SHARKS?

Overfishing and bycatch are by far the biggest threats to sharks. Overfishing is catching too many fish at once, so the breeding population can't properly recover. Bycatch is closely tied to overfishing—it's the capture of unwanted animals while fishing for a different species.

Pollution, climate change, and shark finning are some of the other big threats facing these animals. About 32 percent of the world's sharks and rays are threatened with extinction according to the International Union for Conservation of Nature's Red List of Threatened Species, with ray species found to be at a higher risk than sharks.

HOW IS CLIMATE CHANGE GOING TO IMPACT SHARKS?

Climate change is predicted to have quite an impact on sharks! Changes to migratory patterns, food availability, and even altered brain development are all predicted as our oceans continue to change due to climate change.

HOW CAN WE HELP SHARKS?

Here are some good ways to help:

- How we talk about animals matters. Talk to your friends about how cool and important sharks are!

- Question everything. Does a story or headline seem really scary? Do some research and see what the real truth is.

- Donate your allowance/birthday money to organizations that study and protect our oceans.

- When you grow up and can, volunteer with organizations that study and protect our oceans.

LEARN SPANISH WITH THE VILLALOBOS FAMILY!

- Abuela = grandmother

- Abuelos = grandparents

- Azul = blue

- Basta = enough

- Brillante idea = brilliant idea

- Buenos días, mija = good morning, daughter

- Familia = family

- Hermano = brother

- Hombres = men

- ¡Levántate! = Get up!/Wake up!

- ¡Lo tengo! = I've got it!

- Mamá, puedes decirme otra vez? = Mom, can you tell me again?

- Mamá/Mami = mother

- Mi cariño = my darling

- Mija = my daughter

- Mijo = my son

- Moneda = coin
- Papá/Papi = father
- Tienes que escucharme = you need to listen to me
- Traje de baño = swimsuit
- Vámonos = Let's go

USEFUL PHRASES IN SRI LANKA

- Amma = mother

- Ayubowan = long life (the word used in Sri Lanka to greet someone)

- karaunaākara = please

- Kohomada? = How are you?

- Suba davask! = Have a nice day!

TURN THE PAGE FOR A SNEAK PEEK AT ADRIANNA'S CROCODILE ADVENTURE!

As we sat down for lunch, I shot a glance over at my brother, and then to Mr. Savage. I wiggled my eyebrows in the universal signal for "Should I ask him about the Mega Croc?" Feye nodded slightly.

"Hey, Mr. Savage?" I started.

He looked up at me, wiping his mouth with a napkin. "Yes, Adrianna?" he asked.

"Can you tell us more about this Mega Croc?"

I could tell my dad wanted to interject because his mouth opened up, but it quickly shut when Mr. Savage waved at him and chuckled. "Of course I can!" He began to tell us how the locals have been talking about a massive crocodile that could be a hybrid between the American crocodile, like the injured one we were looking for, and the Cuban crocodile.

"It isn't totally out of the question," our dad hesitantly told Mr. Savage when he was done with his tale. "The Cuban crocodiles are losing their genetic identity because they're interbreeding with the more abundant cousin, the American crocodile."

We had heard about Cuban crocodiles before. Some family friends had seen them in the wild before and were terrified—one said it was like looking at a devil because of their raised eyebrow ridges and dark eyes.

"The Cuban crocodiles could once be found roaming all throughout Cuba but are now only found in large numbers in the Zapata Swamp," my mom added.

"The cameras aren't rolling, you know," Feye joked. Mom stuck her tongue out and we all laughed.

"Now you've said it yourself! The genes of

two dangerous predators mixed into one super-aggressive crocodile," Mr. Savage exclaimed, his drink slamming down onto the table for emphasis as he talked. "Maybe the injured crocodile got into a tussle with the Mega Croc!"

I could see my mom frowning.

"Do you think the injured croc has died?" asked Feye.

"No, I don't think it did. It may be hiding, though. Lying low," said our dad.

Suddenly, all our radios crackled to life as someone said, "*¿Están ustedes allí?* Are you guys there? We have a crocodile sighting! *¡Vemos un cocodrilo!*"

Our mother grabbed the nearest radio. "We're here. Where is it?"

"It's near your boat hotel! And it is HUGE!!" the voice said.

I gasped. Could this be one of the crocodiles we were looking for?

Known as the "Mother of Sharks," Melissa Cristina Márquez is a Latina marine biologist who has a lot of labels: science communicator, conservationist, author, educator, podcaster, and television presenter. Born in Puerto Rico and raised all over the world, she now calls Australia home. She studies sharks, climbs up sand dunes, spies on birds in the rain forest, and tracks down kangaroos in the Outback . . . and then writes about her adventures! Find Melissa online at melissacristinamarquez.com.